Frigid Tales

Frigid Tales

Pedro de Jesús

Translated from the Spanish
by Dick Cluster

City Lights Books
San Francisco

Cuentos frigídos © 1998 by Pedro de Jesús López Acosta
English translation by Dick Cluster © 2002 by City Lights Books
Originally published as *Cuentos frígidos (Maneras de obrar en 1830)* by
Olalla Ediciones, Madrid, 1998 and by Ediciones UNIÓN, Havana, 2000
Published in the United States by City Lights Books, 2002
10 9 8 7 6 5 4 3 2 1

Cover photograph: Eduardo Hernández Santos, *Sin titulo,* from the
series *Homo Ludens* Copyright © Eduardo Hernández Santos. Courtesy
of Eduardo Hernández Santos
Cover design: Stefan Gutermuth / doubleu-gee
Book design: Nigel French / Small World Productions, San Francisco
Editor: Robert Sharrard

Library of Congress Cataloging-in-Publication Data
Jesús, Pedro de, 1970–
 [Cuentos frígidos, English]
 Frigid Tales / / by Pedro de Jesús ; translated from the Spanish by Dick
Cluster.
 p. cm
 ISBN 0 -87286-399-9
 I. Title.
 PQ7390.J48 C813 2002
 863'.64—dc21
 2002024180

CITY LIGHTS BOOKS are edited by Lawrence Ferlinghetti and Nancy J.
Peters and published at the City Lights Bookstore, 262 Columbus
Avenue, San Francisco, CA 94133. www.citylights.com

For my mother, divine.
For Héctor and Carlos,
too human.

In a word, he was well on the way to restoring his reputation when one morning he was extremely surprised to be awakened by two hands covering his eyes.

—Stendhal, *The Red and the Black*

Contents

Translator's Introduction 11

Instructions for a Single Man 15

The Letter 21

Oh, That Music
  (The Importance of Going On Until the End) 35

How to Act in 1830 43

Images, Questions Re:
  Beautiful Dead Woman 67

The Portrait 83

Translator's Introduction

After an intense interaction with his book, a few e-mails by way of third parties, and knocking on some doors in Havana where he was supposed to be but wasn't, I finally met Pedro de Jesús. We sat down to discuss my draft translation over coffee graciously served to us by his friend in Havana who was putting him up. Pedro had come from the small town of Fomento, in the interior province of Sancti Spiritus, where he lives. I had come from Boston. My friend Fabiola Carratalá, who graciously and meticulously reviewed the translations, had come from a few blocks away. We wanted to put quite a few questions to the author about why this word and why that.

You never know how this kind of meeting will go. Once I had an author walk out of a bedroom, shake my hand, walk back into the bedroom, and never reappear; she refused to answer questions by fax or telephone as well. Pedro, on the other hand, was not only most charming and attentive, but happy to explain, without hesitation, the logic behind the choice of every word. Usually he answered with a list of reasons, rarely fewer than three, sometimes as many as six. Mercury, forget quickness or messenger, we're talking changeability, impossibility that its shape should be defined. Intelligence, like what a spy gives you, because it's a first impression, a first report, shapes everything that follows. *Flácido* because it's the opposite of *rígido*, both the characters and their breathing, you see it's a predicate complement, and so . . .

Here as a more detailed example is what he had to say to us about the title of the collection, *Cuentos frígidos*.

1. It's a reference to Virgilio Piñera's story collection *Cuentos frios* (1956). To suggest this is what Piñera might have written if he'd been free to express his homosexuality in print.

2. It's *frígido* rather than *frío* to indicate the literary and linguistic level of the book. *Frígido* is closer to the Latin root of "cold" than the modern *frío* is. It's elevated. Latinate.

3. Frigid is the opposite of arousing, so it characterizes the narrative technique. Dealing with sex but not exciting or pornographic, you understand.

4. Frigidity is lack of desire for sex. Many of the characters are surrounded by sexual pressure and atmosphere, but they may be going through the motions themselves.

A translator's treasure, no? Except that writers are notorious liars when it comes to explaining our thought processes. We often make up something on the spot, something that *might* be true, but another day we may feel and say something else. Could I project this trait onto the helpful Pedro de Jesús? He insisted that "extremely cold" as such was not part of his meaning, not part of what interested him, that (dictionaries notwithstanding) in Cuba *frígido* had no such meaning—perhaps, I thought, because there was no occasion to say, "It's really frigid out today." Intertextual reference, indicator of semantic register, sexually technical term—*nada más*, that was it and that was all. Some time later, Pedro's first novel was published in Havana, and the copy he sent me finally landed in my hands. *Síbilas en Mercaderes* is the story of two writers who decide to support their habits by telling fortunes in a cafe — one which, on impulse, changes its location from Havana to Paris to St. Petersburg to Kuala Lumpur. The names of the protagonists? *Cálida* and *Gélida:* hot, and icy cold.

In the original Spanish edition, *Cuentos frígidos* had a subtitle as well, *Maneras de obrar en 1830*, the title of the fourth story in the book and also that of a chapter from Stendhal's *The Red and the Black* from which the collection's epigraph came. (English editions render this chapter literally as "Ways of Acting in 1830" or less literally as "Men and Manners in 1830" or "Custom and Behavior in 1830" in editions I've seen.) Those interested in pursuing a literary critic's view of the presence of Stendhal in *Frigid Tales*, as well as the presence of Piñero in the character Virgilio in the opening story and other matters, would do well to consult Emilio Bejel's *Gay Cuban Nation* (Chicago, 2001). As far as words from the horse's mouth, here's the story behind the story according to Pedro de Jesús again:

1. Oh, it's not important in itself at all. It's just that this story unites my book because it contains references to the other stories too.

2. But, of course, it is a reference to Stendhal, and it's intended ironically, you see. Stendhal is always held up as an exemplar of realism, and that particular chapter is a description of manners in a given class, time, and place — while in this book I fracture realistic narrative — did any of this "really" happen, at all?

3. But, in truth, I myself don't see Stendhal as realistic in fact . . .

This last explanation led to a disquisition on Stendhal and romanticism which reminded me that I was dealing with a graduate of the University of Havana's formidable *Facultad de Letras* (School of Humanities, or of Language and Literature, or of *belles lettres*, as you wish). Passionate, convincing, but again I asked myself, suspiciously, is this all? *Obrar*, besides "to act," means to have a bowel movement, in about the same euphemistic register as that English term. The "1830" is a fancy Havana seaside restaurant in a mansion originally built with graft money by a 1920s politician for his mistress, and lately become a foreign tourist hangout and pickup spot. No, said Pedro de Jesús with utmost sincerity, none of that occurred to me at all.

So a translator's conversation with Pedro de Jesús is something like one of his stories: mercurial in many senses of the word. Much is said out loud about the process of writing, about the words behind the words, and at the same time the translator is left scratching his head, asking whether or not he has been had. The disquisition on Stendhal and romanticism, nonetheless, helped confirm for me the way *I'd* been reading the book, and that was a happy meeting of minds. Because for me, underneath all of the above, this is a collection of stories about the pursuit of love.

Dick Cluster
Cambridge, Massachusetts, 2001

Instructions for a Single Man

For Lázaro, zapadora

1. Make him come back. Like someone traveling from one vacuum to another. Like someone who has hardly ever moved.

2. Place yourself so you face the evidence, the same objects, and the same disorder.

3. Make her sit in her usual chair, sighing, and wait for something extraordinary that allows for a story.

4. Maneuver a minimal event, almost a trick: Virgilio's arrival.

5. Be infinitely happy. Show it.

6. Set us to talking about loneliness in a way that moves us from the general to the particular. As if anyone's loneliness were unique.

7. Drag them to a tautological confession: to say they are alone.

8. Make you see—you out there—that the characters' needs touch on the metaphysical. As if their consciousness of loneliness stole their bodies in one swift stroke.

9. Grant Virgilio the opportunity to see a tentative way out and to communicate it to us. Then send him off, as if it were all a revelation, or a gift, whose effect was to leave us once more alone.

10. With this insistence on the part of Virgilio, allow yourself to feel motivated to dial the phone number of that underground agency to which others like you resort, communicating their descriptions, their desires, and their needs.

11. Describe myself, convert myself into someone's ideal. Then describe my ideal man. So this ear will know it, so you out there will know it, so I can know it at last.

12. Take care, in this sketch, that this man should be good, sincere, intelligent. Sensitive, mature, responsible. That he should almost not be.

13. Make the voice on the other end demand concreteness, specificity. It should be quite clear, at this point in the plot, that the character has been pushed into declaring himself in favor of fair skin, medium height (or, better yet, tall), and voluminous muscles to be shown off in the street or in the sack. Age may vary between twenty-five and forty.

14. And then you feel moved to add: beautiful, not too flaming, sexually open and daring, and possessed of a cock somewhere between normal and lethal.

15. But: Make us shut up. All of us shut up. For fear of a thunderous collapse of the metaphysical aura.

16. Think—you out there—that the character is racist and frivolous. Get her to inflict such adjectives on herself, once she's hung up the phone. Create an atmosphere of pathos around the affair. Lead the character to a memorable *to be or not to be*.

17. Make me wait for two different men: the good man and the beautiful one. As if waiting always implied the loss of one of the two.

18. Maneuver another event: the call—reply—date from the agency.

19. Dress him inch by inch, as if in tattoos from head to toe. Send him off to his encounter with the man who has given his name as René.

20. Induce them to arrive before René, identify themselves

with the code name Pedro de Jesús, sit down at the tiny round table in the middle of the small, elegant room to which they are solemnly led … and to wait, sipping a Cuba Libre on the house.

21. Maintain your equanimity when you see Virgilio, well decked out, and the oh-so-friendly young man from the agency announces, "Pedro de Jesús, we are delighted to introduce you to René. René, we are delighted to introduce you to Pedro de Jesús."

22. Be overcome by sadness. But I don't show it.

23. Smile when the young man leaves. Take it all as a joke, a revelation, or a favor that leaves us, once again, alone.

24. Have Virgilio declare: "I never knew, till now, that we were each other's ideal."

25. Everyone in agreement, yourself included.

26. Have Virgilio add: "But it's obvious: we're not really look-ing for our ideal men."

27. Agreement again—us, I don't know about yourself.

28. They pretend that they are beginning to get acquainted, that the date is a success. Get drunk. Spend too much. Pay the agency's bill. Leave.

29. Come back. Like someone returning from one vacuum to another. Like someone who has hardly ever moved.

NOTE: Don't write the story. Not that one, nor any other. Give up the vice.

The Letter

Enter the dancer. Till now I'd been able to keep him in the wings, root him out in order to preserve at least the fantasy that what happened to me was not as trivial and common as the histories of others. But the everyday bursts upon us with irresistible force, as my professor of literature likes to say. I'm just one more, in no way different: not even my fingers. Although the rest is absolutely dismal, this is what annihilates me: to figure in a romantic triangle.

Still, if there had been no dancer, there would have been no memory, no capacity to question myself.

I could recite them to the point of exhaustion, those two paragraphs that I never should have written. Neither those, nor the ones that followed. The letter should not have been a letter, a text for others, but rather for me, so as to understand myself and then either love myself or be appalled.

He showed her the pages. He came to her house because she had insulted him.

"I don't understand why you say I insulted you."

I watch him talking: he attracts me. With him is that olive-skinned boy who I don't think is from the college. He seems like a dancer. He's pretty, but ordinary. He on the other hand is every-

thing; his androgyny is unique and he knows how to carry it off so I don't associate it with either sin or guilt. It suits him.

She imagines drowning this body, this so-white skin, in a torrent of water. A shower. I'd love to kiss him all over, in the shower, soap ourselves up so I could slide my hands easily along his back, and close my eyes when my lips have just broken the tiny droplet that was about to fall from his nose. The hotel has run out of water. We're all soapy. Now what would we do?

I try to calm him, always. I find pleasure in protecting him. On the beach I accompany him to take shelter under an umbrella; all day long I share his terror of getting burned. I tried to keep on; he got hysterical.

He started cursing. I wrapped myself in a towel and went out into the corridor. A woman who passed by with a broom looked at me as if I were naked. I didn't have to ask her anything, she just pointed toward two blue tanks at the end of the hall. Every room has a bucket, she explained as she headed down the stairs. I went back in the room, where he was complaining that he had soap in his eyes.

"I'm not 'the dancer,' I have a name, and I'm not even a dancer." He held out the pages of the letter again.

The cubicle cost them a hundred pesos a month. He stole the mattress from the dorm. He knew a negrito who lived on the seventh floor of the building next door. They handed the mattress from one balcony to the other, in the wee hours, so no one would see; then they carried it down, tied and wrapped in a pair of curtains. She, I, was in the street waiting.

The cubicle is close to the dorm, we go on foot. He moves the mattress from one shoulder to the other, and back again. He doesn't want my help, it doesn't weigh anything, it's just awkward is all. He sweats, I see his shirt dampen in the armpits and the back. His chest, not very muscular, is suggestive. His body is a

promise that starts to fulfill itself and then holds back at the cli-
mactic moment and remains postponed. An allusion, a stutter, an
unspoken syllable, but speakable perhaps.

His skin is white. That shouldn't upset him, she likes it that way,
skin which in and of itself requires cleanliness, so washing it be-
comes a daily, necessary, repetition. His body hair is not black;
light coming from behind reveals it as latently blond.

We spread honey on our genitals. She anointed him with this
congealed liquid first. He was disturbed: Hurry is his expression of
fear and anxiety. He wanted to penetrate me with barely a kiss. To
please him, I acceded. I loved him so much. I opened myself to fail-
ure: He couldn't, she always could. I love him so much. I had to
remove the honey with my tongue. Then he coated me and the
dehoneying became mutual. The Fifth Glaciation, my god, with
Heraclitan fire. That's how she defined it, when, after they were
finished, he asked her—a habit—to think over their acts. Or re-
think them? Was there anything between them that wasn't
thought out a priori? *Was there anything spontaneous? Was*
there anything at all? The fire joke fascinated him. He said, that's
why I like you so much.

"I couldn't remember your name. Anyway, it doesn't seem
pejorative to call you that. I thought you were a dancer."

It didn't matter that he was a homosexual, in fact it made him
more interesting. Did he know the Kinsey scale? That's right, the
scale for registering sexual preferences. Great, a stroke of luck,
that he was well-informed because it made it easier to ask him
delicate things. What? His number on the scale. Six, exclusively
homosexual, and a smile of such complicity that I took it for a
joke. It doesn't matter, say I, I'll see to it you change your number
if only by one degree. I'll settle for a five.

They laugh. Five, if he remembers right, is predominantly ho-
mosexual, rarely hetero . . . She agrees. Could she settle for a single

contact, almost accidental, and leave it be, as if life were nothing more? Because the expression "rarely" implies something casual, accidental, by mistake.

No, it would never be a mistake, she was convinced that he'd move from one number to another as soon as he discovered her. He might roll from six all the way to zero, exclusively hetero-sexual. No, no way, he would not devalue himself to that extent. They laughed. I admired his ability to manipulate words, locate them in just the right place. I wanted to go on provoking him.

He didn't think that a zero was truly degraded, did he? Was that her situation, then? Not even a little higher up, not even a "rarely" homosexual? Too bad, him so high on the scale and her so low. Two extremes always meet, I say, and then he's the one who's impressed. They smile, and he continues provoking her.

She should be more careful what she says. If someone heard her they might think she was admitting the equal possibility of her being a zero or a six. . . . In fact, he too was convinced she'd change from one number to another as soon as she found out about him.

Then with him at zero and her at six, they'd be the two ex-tremes again. Everything would be switched. Isn't it beautiful, that someone can stand you on your head and suddenly you're surprised to find that you are what you're not?

"I thought you were a dyke but I never insulted you."

The day before going to live in the cubicle, he managed to sneak her into the dorm. It was the turning point. As soon as the door shuts behind them, both still on their feet, he asks whether I've seen Bertolucci's film Last Tango in Paris. *He always surprises me, in a unique and unrepeatable way.*

Yes. He has his back to her. She is disposed to do anything he asks. She loved him so much. She cuts the fingernails of her right hand, or left, I don't remember, and slides her fingers into his anus, just like that, standing up, in cold blood.

That scene is one she'll never forget. It's stuck in her memory as if, in some way, she had lived it. She would have to live it. She lived it. I am living it. When he mentioned the title, I suddenly felt that the scene was dominating me. Just that one scene.

It was a premonitory scene that had possessed her in secret for the past two years. When the movie ended, she walked and walked and walked, somnambulant, without being able to let go of that image. She had the frightening impression that now she could never go back. Caught in a design that transcended me, for which I was no longer responsible.

That must be what bothers him. That I had guessed his intentions. But he was wrong. Those intentions, really, were not his; they only belonged to me.

She had waited ever since seeing Last Tango in Paris, *for months she waited impatiently to meet him and then seduce him.*

She invited them to the House of Tea and gave them the address of her apartment—both of them, to dispel suspicions. She was afraid he would see the obsession in her fingers, and she kept them hidden beneath the table. Until at last we got up, and there were no more hiding places, and he said, "What pretty hands you've got!" Probably he was talking about her fingers. Can the hand be anything else?

Or maybe I'm the one mistaken, and my intentions were not the same as his.

His intentions perhaps were different, and I let myself be caught. I got lost.

Was it a parody? I'm cutting my nails with my teeth because we don't have any scissors. He's sitting on the cot and he's watching me: He's anxious. I need to file them, I'll hurt him if I don't. It's just by chance that today I brought the emery board along. It was a trick, everything was prepared in advance.

I wash my hands, I want them to be clean. I propose we take a shower, there's water, I need to breathe him in without extraneous odors, absorb the white as part of the smell—a need that sharpens her senses to the extreme and then leaves them paralyzed and her exhausted, slack. I'm nothing but a narcissistic lung that breathes itself in and falls asleep, oblivious to the air around me. I'm a woman fulfilled. I was a woman fulfilled.

The everyday bursts upon us with overwhelming force, concludes the professor, and she fans herself with her legs held apart. María Isabel has recovered the bottle of shampoo that another girl, a fellow student, has reached to her through the barely opened classroom door, in the middle of a passionate speech about the tragic vision of human existence in the works of Racine.

I don't know why I remember that now and smile; I should get furious and demand that he leave, insist I won't accept insults in my own house.

"I see you're not afraid. I thought you were the frustrated type."

That was the max. Him lying down with his back and the soles of his feet on the bed, his knees bent. I can still close my eyes and see him there, with his eyes closed too—so as not to look at me?— open to the possible, perhaps the impossible. No, it was to feel her. If at least she had that certainty, it would mitigate, somewhat, the sense of devaluation that's eating away at her now. With her own saliva she moistened two fingers: first one, then the other.

I, seated between his legs, which were resting on my shoulders. Not a single kiss and, nonetheless, she got goose bumps, she trembled, she lost herself in his depths and sank too into herself. She loved him so much. He, on edge, panting, in paroxysm. I, in paroxysm, panting, on edge. Without a single kiss, it was enough to watch him gyrate, contort himself, move with a part of me, an appendage of mine, inside of him. At last I closed my eyes. I didn't see him. That was my last blindness.

Was it a parody? he asks, but she can't answer. She was mute.

Today she doesn't want to rethink the actions but relive them. It was revolting. A mockery, an allusion of subtle but supreme cruelty. Now, distant from that fullness, I feel an ancestral emptiness and insufficiency. Useless before a man who needs more than I can offer. I'm awash in sick desires to cut off my fingers, to beat them to a pulp. I pity myself. I feel ridiculous.

"I'm not a lesbian, if that's what concerns you. And please, tell me concretely what you came for, don't go on offending me, you don't have any right. You don't know me and, anyway, you're in my house, where I don't have to allow you to ..."

"You knew I existed."

"Look, there's no sense in arguing about that, now that my thing with him is done."

"Then why did you send the letter?"

"The letter wasn't for you."

"It was for him, that's almost the same. And he gave it to me. Between us two, everything is the same again as before you interfered. You have no right to say, 'Enter the dancer.' I was never lost, never disappeared from his life."

"He told me you had broken up."

"You never knew anything. He used you."

We drank so as to wipe out all pacts and all goals, so as to avoid having to suffer the horrors of our intersection. His eyes were red, yes, before crying. They were red from the soap that got in them when the water ran out. After crying he didn't have eyes, not then, not later, never—so as not to look at me? She too was growing blind, inoculated by the darkness, a virus. Always at night, always at the mercy of the elements, except the day of the dehoneying.

I can never get to sleep after trying it and him not being able to. The bulb turned out and the four walls of the cubicle talking among themselves, in growing whispers. The eternal closing in of one wall toward another, the other to the other, the other to the other, the other to the first. Like a mouth pressed to an ear, and that one's mouth incrusted in the next one's ear, and so . . . Crushing us and crushing us until we're reduced to two points on the mattress, on the floor.

They cried. They looked at each other tenderly, you could almost say they were aroused. They were going to embrace. Now she would love him, illuminated by the lamp, hallucinated by his skin which roused her with the barest touch. Every hair of his body, the color of honey in the light shining from behind, would grow firm and erect.

They cried, they were about to embrace. Everything goes dark. The electricity went out in the hotel. I don't even want to remember. I heard him vomiting, he was complaining from the edge of the bed. We ended up masturbating, each one with their back to the other.

"It doesn't matter now. I was happy, and I think he was too. That's what matters."

Lack of satisfaction, is that the cause? she asks within the four walls of that cubicle, with the incandescent bulb lit at last. Doesn't he know that no one will ever understand his sexual behavior, so unpredictable and unbalanced? No, not the homosexuality, that she understood. She spoke of his periods of impotence, of his growing introspection that spoiled the tenderness of the beginning. She spoke of the passivity with which he'd started taking the relationship. And didn't she like that any more? She had always seemed very happy making love to him; it was her, practically, who was always possessing him. Did it never occur to her that he could feel an inferiority complex and imagine her unsatisfied?

She didn't defend herself. He left, forever.

I feel sorry for him. I love him so much. Everything started to go wrong once the mattress appeared there on the floor. I contradict myself: I don't know if it was then, or before, or always. His par-

ents, as soon as they learned he had a girlfriend, right away they gave him money to rent the room. I think I was the only woman they knew about; he didn't tell me whether I was the first. He never talked seriously. I think I was, I was the first, because he didn't know how to act, he was trembling.

She was on top. That became our position. We had been talking for hours, and the night had grown so dark, with no moon. The moon is tragic, he said. Impossible for me to resist the excitement that every word or gesture of his provoked. That delicacy and defenselessness were so unique, just his presence made me captive to a maternal instinct I hadn't known I had.

We're seated on moist, sticky ground. The sharpness of the coral bothers him and instead we've picked a spot higher up, between the wall and the slope.

She begins, kisses him, feels him. She continues, she shows him, she rumples his hair, she mounts him. She loves him so much.

He has put a kerchief on the ground so as not to soil his pants. When they get up he stretches the strip of cloth before his eyes, examines it carefully, confirms the stain. He's nervous. She holds him by the waist. He puts the cloth away and wraps his arms around her shoulders.

Enter the dancer. Till now I'd been able to keep him in the wings, root him out in order to preserve at least the fantasy that what happened to me was not as trivial and common as the histories of others. But the everyday bursts upon us with irresistible force . . .

I could recite to the point of exhaustion what I never should have written, the letter that should not have been a letter, a text for others, but rather for me, to understand myself and then love myself or be appalled.

"The letter wasn't for you."

"It was for him, that's almost the same. And he gave it to me. Between us two, everything is the same again as before you interfered. You have no right to say, 'Enter the dancer.' I was never lost, never disappeared from his life."

I felt happy, I'd finally gotten hold of the videotape of Last Tango in Paris, *now I only needed to find someone with a VCR. Was I getting obsessive?*

Since everything ended, it's as if it hadn't happened. I don't know him, everything is ready to begin.

I walked and walked and walked, somnambulant, without being able to let go of that image. I had the frightful impression that now I could never go back. Caught in a design that transcended me, for which I was no longer responsible.

I could recite to the point of exhaustion . . .

I saw them, the two of them, in that darkened park—an ordinary place—kissing. No, it wasn't the two of them. She was mistaken. She walked and walked, somnambulant, without being able to let go of that image.

I could recite to the point of exhaustion.

"He told me you two had broken up."

"You never knew anything. He used you."

"It doesn't matter now. I was happy, and I think he was too. That's what matters."

"He never loved you. He wouldn't have given me the letter to return to you."

I'm awash in sick desires to cut off my fingers, to beat them to a pulp. I pity myself. I feel ridiculous.

"No, go away. Tear it up."

"You do it, that would be the best way to accept that it's all over."

He gets up, leaves the letter there, on the couch. He's at the door, he's going to open it, he opens it and turns: "Oh, I forgot the most important thing. I'm supposed to tell you to find out for sure your number on the Kinsey scale."

He closes the door slowly.

Enter the dancer. Till now I'd been able to keep him in the wings, root him out in order to preserve at least the fantasy that what happened to me was not as trivial and common as the histories of others. But the everyday bursts upon us with irresistible force . . .

"I could recite to the point of exhaustion . . ."

Oh, That Music
(The Importance of Going On Until the End)

There's strange music. Cultivated, outsized fingers, worthy of piano-man or class-A typist, seem to direct harmonies of most intimate orchestra, oscillation between *pianissimo* most delicate and most strident *fortissimo.*

Him, seated on sand, skimpiest bikini brief, sun baking him like a brick. Cigarette, vertical, spattered with sun lotion, dangles miraculously from digital spasm, resisting, too, gusts of wind.

Insistent glances, symphonic play of hands, and I like his body: I accept invitation to accompany him home.

Body: prominent bulges, equity, grace.

Home: I don't describe it, because only body interests me. Not even music on record player, absolute redundancy.

(Temptation to change this story. If it were possible, I would write: "I feel lonely. I've come to the beach to convince myself someone can like me. I discover him, he discovers me, and we decide to go to his place."

Put that way, it would sound simple, and it's not. I would speak of fear of failure, of my vague hope in this man. I would describe the folding chairs, the small stained table, the electric hot plate, the Madonna poster, the dusty stairs up to the home-made loft. It would be prolix, would attempt to portray those scant twenty square meters with the minute detail of one harboring the dream of coming back one more time to corroborate that they continue to exist. It would be stupid.)

Allow touch on occasion, chest or thigh, his shyness too controlled, simulating musical beat, or note requiring movement of hands. For sure, thinks it is too soon to let sound pistol shot in middle of concert. Speaks of heat, latest Michael Jackson scandal, country's economic plight. I keep quiet, touch with more daring, suggest happiness is a warm gun, pinch nipple within reach, or back of right hand explores left flank until arrives border of ass. He's aroused, I perceive lively penis under shorts.

When tries to bring mouth to lips, push him away, fastidiousness, and smile. Terrified by disaster, he stands up and jokes:

"You're like these kerosene stoves: you heat up but you don't cook."

Shuts off record and goes to refrigerator and glancing about in search of something, intones melody:

He let me down.
He let me down.
He told me he was a "top"
Then turned around
Then turned around.

(Need to include a speech by me—is this a theater piece?—that tells him his attitude belongs in an old story, from the forties or fifties, repeated and disguised until it has lost the capacity to move or surprise us; this is a new, *novísimo* story and he should think and act in another way. But I have no right to force him to participate in a different story. Everyone is free to choose his own. Better a dialogue—so, is this a short story?—in which I confess my dreams and fears. It would go like this:

"It's not the question of active or passive that worries me, but how ephemeral this encounter."

"Tell me, my love, what time machine did you emerge from?"

That would be awful. I would see at a stroke that the old and the new are relative concepts. And then how could the story or theater piece go on?)

I have to laugh. I laugh.

"Do you like Amanda Miguel?" he asks, features nearly rigid, jaw tight, plate of coleslaw in hand, standing straight.

"No, I like your version," I lie.

He sits down after placing plate on table, finish tattooed in perfect circles by glasses cold rum or hot tea.

Silence.

Actor opens legs, leans down, supports elbows on thighs, links hands to form fist that supports head by chin. Opens legs more, unlinks knotted hands, and arms fall on thighs. Bends head some and shakes it, denying something. Very serious, voice grave, discordant noise, roars out line:

ACTOR 1: Shit man, why didn't you say I was El Macho in this movie?

ACTOR 2: (Has to laugh. Laughs.) You're right for the part.

(Suddenly I don't know whether this is a story, a theater piece, or a film. Whatever it is, I'd like to criticize myself for the inconsistency of continuing to participate in something of which I disapprove. I criticize myself. And go on.)

Actor 1, without allowing Actor 2 to finish, puts feet together, leans back in chair, small turn on *gluteus maximus* to allow sidelong glance, crosses legs, hands rest on top knee, five fingers stretch upward, arch, then move one by one at typing or pianoplaying speed. I hear strange music.

Blinks in time with hands, shows whites of eyes, puckers lips as if to make kiss-kiss middle of La Rampa cruising ground. Seconds only like that, uncrosses legs and separates, just slightly, rests hands on seat, still. I watch him deflate, take a deep breath, so I tremble first time when he confesses:

"This is all a bad act. It was you who slid your hand as far as my ass and probably you wanted to touch my cock. (Transition)

Do you want some coleslaw? It's all I've got."

"The coleslaw is just another act, and your little song," I attack. "You're trying to disguise your disappointment that I rejected you."

ACTOR 1 (Indignant, nearly yelling): "What do you want me to say? (Stands up and sits back down) That I need a cock? (Pause. Tension. Drama) No, I need a person, a human being ... (Pause, Tension, Drama) Who has a cock, yes, because I like cocks. If not, I wouldn't be a queer!"

(Need to stop the action to ask him to remain like that, eternally repeating the word "need." Need someone. The image would freeze and a voice from *off* would utter the phrase in time with the opening of his mouth. Those words of his and the rage with which he pronounces them convert us into characters in a story that could be written in any century, without labels. We would kiss at last. Freeze-frame dissolves, successive takes. I'd describe the kiss. And then I'd speak of his body, his immense back, the dark birthmark on his abdomen, the thighs without adjectives, the firm cheeks of his ass, his gland even firmer, his toes, his pierced earlobe, his tongue with the taste of nicotine. I'd even allow myself a humoristic slip, adapting Martí: "The *glottis* moist as a clitoris, but better that it's not, because if it is a clitoris, I don't know, I can't go in." I would speak of his esophagus, his lungs, his viscera. I'd affirm: "I want to make a mark on his life forever, just as the glasses have on the varnish of the table." There would be music in the background. It would be beautiful, magnificent. But I don't know whether the anger is real, if he's saying words he's learned, if behind the unfreezing of the frame comes beauty or horror. I'm afraid of these images. Nonetheless, the short story or film or theater piece has to go on. Always.)

"I too need a person, a human being." I decide to make that a voice from *off*, reluctant, so he won't believe.

"And a cock?" Question with same ferocity as Actor 1 last speech.

He gets to his feet, midstage, and without waiting for Actor 2 response, takes off shorts, throws them on table next to cole-slaw, and audience sees cock. It's beauteous. Of such antique beauty for the eyes, that the tongue cannot find contemporary words: beauty now extinct.

ACTOR 2 (I keep using phrases identical to those of Actor 1— getting myself off the hook, prolonging the freeze-frame so the story never has to end?): "I need a person with a cock, that's why I'm queer, all right?"

ACTOR 1 (Declamatory and ironic): "Then there's no problem. We both have what we had to have . . ."

ACTOR 2 (Air of great wisdom and depth): "You've got very interesting tastes: Amanda Miguel, Nicolás Guillen. From the crocus to the lily . . ."

(Desire not to be pedantic and to sing, too, Amanda Miguel, Lucía Méndez, Ana Gabriel, something light, not this crushing gravity, this density that makes it impossible to construct a simple story.)

"That's by a certain . . . I don't remember. . . . A lover would read me that poem every time he got tragic on me. Come on, you didn't come here to talk poetry and I'm not inclined toward guessing games at this stage. Don't disguise things any further. Take off your shorts. Whatever you are."

(I'm a person. Urge to flee. If I left, he wouldn't feel anything, he'd get dressed again, head for the street with his bronzed skin—divinity to be burned by that heat—and he could conquer all. And me? Another story. Another movie. Another theater piece. I couldn't stand starting over; new beginnings are so difficult, unthinkable after such a good one: "There's strange music," and so on. I need to end it well, although at this point I don't know what a good ending is.)

Seeing fear I must have on face, and perhaps because understands clumsiness of offer, sits in chair, and deliberate voice inquires:

"Why do we complicate life inventing a macho? That doesn't exist any more."

I point out was him first brought up subject. Presses thigh to thigh and whispers, lucidity surprising and suspicious:

"Excuse me. All the men who have passed through here have been in search of a macho. They don't find him and always end up blaming me for their loss. That's why, every time one comes, I try to blame him first. It's a ghost I can't manage to wipe out, although I want to."

I want to tell him I bring along other ghosts, different ones. But it's better to get to the ending as fast as possible, without delays. I accept defeat: I'm always unsatisfied with story and can't do anything to switch directions. I swivel eyes toward record player—empty—and nonetheless think I hear violin Kansas, *All we are is dust in the wind.*

"It's okay with me," and that's all I say.

"Me too." And all he says?

We even smile, and I'm dropping my shorts and the brief little by little. He looks at my penis and I watch him watching me: I'm getting aroused; I look at his penis and he watches me watching him: he's getting excited. We stand up and we press one against the other, hot. It's strange music, and fascinating. We hold each other tightly, tightly, around the waist and softly bite each other's lips.

(Nobody can change this story.)

How to Act in 1830

Six months after the publication of my story "The Letter," I received a middle-sized package, an envelope, carefully sealed with rubber band, tape, and staples. The exaggerated tendency toward the hermetic, joined with absence of any identification of the sender, accorded to the act of tearing open the envelope a nearly trembling avidity that I still remember well. I managed only to destroy it.

The many sheets of paper within were typewritten and unsigned, all of which intensified the mystery of the affair, and my curiosity. The first sheet contained a short note in which the anonymous individual praised "The Letter" and confessed that the act of reading it had corroborated a "very powerful intuition" about my destiny as a "great writer" which the sender had formed when we were both adolescents and studied together in the same class.

She—it was a woman—also did some writing, but she considered herself lacking in imagination. Absolutely all her stories were "autobiographical and/or real," and for this reason it was difficult for her to show them to anyone. Now, halfway overcoming her scruples, she was sending me one of these stories, in which she had changed the names of people and places in order to avoid being recognized. She requested that I read it and then, if it were not too much trouble, send her my opinion of the story, to any of the three post office boxes listed below.

Apologizing for her anonymity, she explained that the possibility of making a fool of herself with her stories frightened her. In any case, she ended the note, I could call her Madame Rénal or Julien Sorel, or even Matilde: She was not opposed to romantic triangles, nor was she at all like the character in "The Letter."

Underneath her signature she added a postscript in which she confessed to being very bad at titles and asked me to propose one for her "story"—within quotation marks, like that.

I immediately turned the page and began to read:

Yesterday I was trying to sleep, and through the slatted windows of my room I heard moans, high-pitched cries, low-pitched ones, and moans again. Sitting up in my bed, with my arms wrapped around my legs, I listened coldly, reducing my being to those sounds.

Even without participating in the act, I had to be moved by it. It was a challenge. I tried to masturbate at the expense of these sounds. I could recognize every one of the couple's movements and positions according to the variation of their voices; I was absolutely certain as to each event of their amatory adventures. It was so easy to imagine them. But I didn't get aroused.

When they finished, both of them supine upon the mattress, facing each other, sweat-drenched, exhausted, I began to masturbate, recognizing my own body, in silence, so that no one could guess.

This goes on daily. I'm surrounded. Rebeca and Alicia live two floors down; in the floor above, passionate and even noisier, a black man and a mulatta; across the way, a precious boy with blue eyes, white skin, and blond hair. Tato goes through stretches without nocturnal visits, but when he's on a good streak, I can hear his lovers stuffing a pillow in his mouth to muffle his screams. Sometimes that's not enough, and he ends up biting their wrists. One time he sank his teeth into the shoulder of his lover of the moment, which set off a racket that kept me awake the rest of the night.

So I live bearing witness to my neighbors' lives so as to compare them to my own. It's a vice, and a damaging one. I vow not to be pathetic, talking about this, but I am—from start to finish. How could I not be?

Tomorrow I'm going to Camagüey, to see my family and the house which little by little has ceased to be mine, to walk the streets which, for knowing them so well, I don't recognize, and to see people who I wish would disappear. The only welcome thing is Laura. And not even her.

She knows I'm coming, she'll wait for me in the train station. She'll come in lightweight short-shorts and an oversize T-shirt whose lower hem just coincides with that of the pants. She'll seem naked. That precise nakedness that she practices and I used to admire so much. We'll kiss, effusively, and hug slow and tight. This embrace is what survives.

We spent years sleeping in a dark cubicle populated by couples like us. For the rest of them, what mattered was company in the middle of the night, a defense against the looks and touches of the intruders who sneaked into the dorm. For us, though, it wasn't our fear but our need. We fell asleep stroking each other's arms, face, thighs, or bellies, with our fingertips or with our nails. We competed to see who could grow them longest, and keep them so.

Tomorrow Laura will help me with my suitcase, we'll tie

it to her bicycle rack, then I'll get on behind, and she'll take me to her house. That's as habitual as the sounds that surround me here. Another vice. Laura will wait till I've eaten something to begin explaining her quarrels with Carlos. She'll ask for advice. I'll eat and listen. Such a long and repetitious story no longer attracts me; it breaks off and then it grows back with a strange and eternal regenerative power like that of fingernails.

Now our game is who can have them shorter. The competition annoys me and at the same time it seduces me. She always wins. I let her win, it pleases me to surrender to the invariable punishment: The loser has to narrate her latest sexual event.

I always cheated her, though my purpose back then was to avoid having to hear the details of her intimate life with her boyfriends. I couldn't stand her prolix, almost pornographic descriptions; they gave rise to enormous envy, and powerlessness. I was a virgin, and my ignorance made me feel inexpert and incompetent. I told her the only thing I could: my latest masturbation, always a fantasy, latest dream. Ridiculous.

Now it's not like that. It's very agreeable wearing her out with outlandish sexual sagas of which I am the protagonist. I feign embarrassment so she won't catch on to my trick. I exaggerate my sexual episodes and use these as a starting point for others; I show I can teach her and dominate her.

This time I'll describe the sexual act between Rebeca and Alicia, as if I were Alicia. It won't be any trouble to put myself in their places, to narrate the main chain of events: the kisses, the hands, the angles, fingers, nipples, tongue . . . I'll include the cries and groans, but give them a secondary place (it's terrible to accept that this is what I live on, the secondary), and I'll put myself into my perspective too, I can do that, I'll be an anonymous ear that Rebeca and I can sense in a certain moment of the act, that causes us to bite each other furiously to strangle our cries. Rebeca had to resort to the pillow because, in my pain, I started to pound my fists into her back. Afterward we fought. I'll reconstruct the fact of the blond boy who lives across from me. I don't know whether I used his history already in another of my fictions, but it will work again, with variation. The secret lies in transforming the experiences of others so they seem different, and mine. Laura, even if she's heard them before, will act joyful, interested, surprised. Sometimes I think she's my accomplice in the game; sometimes not. I'm confused.

I confronted that text, believing in its autobiographical and realistic character beyond the shadow of a doubt. It was a *striptease* (almost gossip) performed by someone I had known and about whom I now, suddenly, possessed very intimate details. Although I found it well written, without many frills or resort to purple prose, I could hardly discuss such stylistic questions, much less keep reading. The consciousness that the first paragraphs testified to a concrete life, outside of themselves, impelled me to dissect them over and over again, searching for evidence to corroborate or refute the many hypotheses which I developed as to the identity of that life.

I threw the "story" aside to send a brief note the author:

Madame Rénal:
Impossible to express an opinion about your tale. I need to know who you are. Why don't you show me the original, with the true names of the people and places? Be brave, take full responsi-

bility for autobiography and realism, wherever they lead. Don't flirt with them.

Stendhal

Then I went right back to reading:

Even when I lost the fingernail competition, Laura would end up stuffing my head with her sexual conquests. All my strategies were useless, only making things worse. But not now: now Laura revels in confessing her contra- dictions and failures to me. Often I interpret the change as a sign of pity, that she lies because she sympathizes with my inferiority. Other times, I think it's a device of hers to bring us closer.

The last time I went to Camagüey, Laura asked me to make love. In spite of my surprise, I didn't say anything. I had never imagined she could go to bed with another woman. I tried to get control of myself, I took my clothes off, she'd already done hers while we were talking. To hold her in a new way. Go further than our adolescent custom. I couldn't tell whether or not I really wanted this, or whether I'd been longing for it so much that my fear of rejection made the desire disappear. Why had Laura decided on it? I was clumsy and unable to get free of the flow of my thoughts even for an instant. She kissed me, touched me, and what did I do? Nothing — I watched her push on, asking me with her fingers and with her eyes, what was the way, Claudia, I knew more about sex between women, I should tell her, please. I pulled away. Laura asked whether I was attracted to her. Awful. I didn't respond.

When I got back to Havana, Jorge Ángel was waiting for me in the train station. I hardly said hello. He asked, insistently, about my weekend. I said I'd slept for the whole seventy-two hours. My annoyance was evident. We had no commitment to be faithful to each other, yet Jorge Ángel dreamed of formalizing our relationship. He pursued me with flowers, sweets, cheaply grandiloquent letters, and the ugliest clay figures, which he made himself. I was alarmed by how lovestruck he was, and I abused him throughout.

Jorge Ángel, though, was a formidable man in bed. That was all I asked of him. His long-lasting erections exalted me. He suffered from retarded ejaculation, I think. We had hours of mutual extermination.

No, it's all over. It's over. It's over. I've repeated this many times but apparently not often enough. He perseveres. The last time, he accused me of being a lesbian; the rumor was already running through the dorm from one end to the next. I didn't deny my contacts with women. Astounded, he asked whether I was attracted to him, whether he turned me on. I wavered. I was afraid that being frank would raise his hopes, but I felt that sincerity was the appropriate thing. Yes, you turn me on. And more: a lot.

He didn't understand a simultaneous attraction to men and women. I explained: it's not women and men, but certain women and certain men. I added: It's not always at the same time, it might be at different times. He still didn't understand. Was I sure I was attracted to him? I didn't say anything, I couldn't abide his disbelief. What parts of his body turned you on, Claudia? His penis, his thighs, his chest, his mouth. Him.

While I was saying this I experienced desires to reach out and kiss the parts I was naming. I got him to undress, standing up, startled, handsome. Without a hair to hide his hard muscles, his taut skin. I get goose bumps just remembering. I touched him all over, slowly, almost imperceptibly. I touched him urgently, pressing and squeezing, his skin instantly recovering its smoothness. I adored this smoothness, yet felt incited to blemish it.

We kissed. We made love and afterward he pretended to fall asleep. He needed to stay with me that night. I guessed his intentions and pretended to wake him up. He rubbed his eyes. Go away, I stammered. He sat up on the bed, his bare feet on the clean floor, his naked behind on the dirty sheet. Go away, I repeated. Again questions, complaints, supplications. A round NO, without explanation: Go away.

A few days later, Jorge Ángel was proclaiming my lesbianism in every corner. He had joined the choir. One more.

That woman fascinated me. About somebody like her, I would have written a brilliant story, maybe the one I was missing. That we had coincided in place and time, yet I didn't know her, seemed a crime. All the bygone faces that my mind unearthed refused to belong to her. Luckily, an answer came quickly, in a small envelope:

My dear Stendhal:
Not even Stendhal himself could have done so, or wanted to. In my case, if you read the history carefully, "I live by these lies." That's the only thing strictly autobiographical and/or realistic in it. If I decided to show you the "story" under conditions of anonymity, I was because I thought you could rise above them. In spite of your curiosity, I still think so, and I wait.

Sincerely,
Julien Sorel

This disconcerted me. I didn't know whether to see these words as aggressive or elegant, to consider the situation a joke or something quite serious. I was so attached to the idea of a true confession that the statements in the letter disappointed me a bit. Did the pages have any value aside from what my original belief conferred on them? Conquering the annoyance they now provoked, I looked at them again:

> For almost two months, several lesbians in the dorm had begun to coalesce into a strident clan that then grew vertiginously, to the point of including girls from outside the world of the university. For their expansive powers and the aggressivity they projected, they were baptized The Vikings. They were the scandal of the moment. They could be found in the front hall of the building at any hour, or on the stairway, or the sidewalk, or up in the bedrooms too. They were ubiquitous, and their partying, constant.

> I hovered around their edges while I could. The afternoon following my return from Camagüey, Nancy, a well-known Viking with whom I had maintained quite a stormy relationship some while before, invited me to drink a few bottles of rum with the group. Without any erotic intentions implied, she made clear.

> The proposition was a challenge. From our previous arguments, I knew that Nancy disapproved of my silence about my sexual life. She had accused me of fear and self-repression. I had rebutted her, explaining that, if indeed I was intolerant of the permanent confession and exhibitionism demanded by the others in order to accept one as a person realized in sex —and if this conviction on my part precluded public proclamations of intimate affairs— nonetheless I did not seek absolute secrecy about them, which was an absurd goal in our dorm, a place so given to

the pleasures of "communication." It was just that I resisted collaboration with the culture of the hawker's chant and its more modern substitute, the neon sign.

Of course, I didn't confess that with Laura I tried to show off and even exaggerate my "advances" in matters of sex. I never spoke to Nancy about this apparent incoherence. Would she have understood that, for me, it was as if Laura were the world and through her ears I cried out what the world longed to hear?

I accepted the invitation without hesitation. Firmly. To convince her I wasn't afraid. I felt a childish desire to strut my stuff, to enter myself in evidence. I put my arms around Nancy's shoulders and, to suggest a certain intimacy, whispered something unintelligible in her ear. She smiled without understanding and gave me a brusque slap on the ass. We went to the group, who were posted on the front sidewalk, and she introduced me to those I didn't know, who that day were only two: Rocky and La Bombón. The one doesn't either study or work, and the other dances in a nightclub: a couple. I kissed them dramatically and loud. I was introduced, in Nancy's words, as a freelance dyke.

I kept acting. I'm capable of being histrionic in a way that manages to confuse everyone, or almost everyone, including myself. Once I let loose, I lose consciousness of what I am. It's like a mask that can't be removed without destroying the face that's holding it up. Maybe they're right, the ones who claim that the mask is a brace for the face, and maybe the face is the first mask, or not the first. Maybe it's true that the only reality is unlimited theatricality, and that masks don't hide anything but, rather, constitute the only way to reveal anything, the supreme evidence.

At this point, I wonder who I am. Who. I'm not clear to myself.

Am I the one who moves in on Rocky, to whom I've just been introduced, and asks what number she is, Rocky IV or Rocky V, and is she a professional boxer or amateur, and could I last a round with her? Am I the one who suggests a tasting of La Bombón, a little taste whether strawberry or chocolate, where are you hiding it, why not take it out so we can share this tasty candy among us all?

Am I the one who doubles over in laughter, who enlivens the group with jokes as soon as I appear, her jokes, that one who I'm not sure is me; the one who, while pointing without reserve toward the dorm with her finger, makes it clear that she knows that from every balcony everybody is asking, right now, which of the two, you or La Bombón, is the female and which is the male?

Am I the one who asks, please Bombón, hug Rocky now, be the man of the streets, be the *ñáñigo* of the secret rites; and you, Rocky, please, let yourself be hugged, stylize yourself, flutter your lashes, stamp your heel? Am I the one who asks them, please, switch roles and switch again, drive them crazy, those eternal watchers, so they'll never know who's the female and who's the male?

Am I the one who, when La Bombón protests and says in fact they are neither way, and what they are is fantastic, tough, tasty, tropical females, stresses that it's a joke—didn't they realize?—and that to play and be effective it's necessary to make use of the enemy's code?

They don't understand about the game, the code, and the adversary; I'm threading words into phrases learned in the other world, the university, foreign phrases now mine. Am I that one who appropriates these phrases and uses them believing they are hers?

I'm always getting trapped by false disjunctions. As if my life had been a long, wide road that suddenly, in a time I no longer remember, changed into many narrow shortcuts, entangled and scattered, and the design of my existence consisted in discovering and exploring all of them, happily, without worrying, reveling in such plurality and diversity—only to once in a while, and with a truly atavistic trembling, feel myself out of place and astray in an irreversible tangle, and to begin suffering nostalgia for that wide and long and only road, which one day could have been my life. As if I were dead. Or cast into an intermediate state somewhere between life and death.

Too many details. Too ambitious and monotonal. But a devilish individuality ran through it. No, I said to myself, no one can make up something so disturbing and so vivid. That passion, that terror, they are real. I felt admiration and even envy for the author, in spite of her literary lapses. I wrote her a desperate missive.

Unforgettable Matilde:

I won't court you, because I am not capable of slipping from six to some other number on the Kinsey scale, as you must know if you know me ("The Letter" is not autobiographical). Nonetheless, I would so much like to meet you, talk with you, hear more stories of your life, that I am, in effect, irretrievably in love. I suspect that you must have known from the beginning what would happen to me, and that you have the denouement of this epistolary game well-prepared. Everything depends on you, my dear. I have fallen fatally into the nets of love, and, reduced to a cipher, can barely marshall the strength to send you this note.

Eternally yours,
I don't know whether Stendhal or Julien Sorel

While I awaited a response, I reread the text:

Despite the lack of enthusiasm for my proposal, I don't shut up. I shield myself in eloquence. From the dorm, they observe how at home in this ambience I am: they whisper, pretend not to be watching, smile; I am the news of the day. From now on I'll be on the receiving end of indiscreet, inquisitive, and mocking glances; I'll attract their rejection, which will be not nearly as subtle as they think. I blush at my starring role —only an instant—and continue my speech.

The door monitor has gone off to the dining hall, so we bring Rocky and La Bombón inside. We climb the stairs to the seventh floor, where we make some food and start to drink.

I like Rocky. She pulls the armchair out from under Virginia when Virginia is about to sit down, and then laughs at the result; that's her code, the number placed after the address or dialed to make a long-distance call. For Rocky, no adversary seems to exist, even when she shoots me glances, openly, in front of La Bombón. They call her Rocky on account of her awkward stride, the aggressive grimace of her mouth, her brusque manner, her dark voice. To me, she suggests the exposure of a small animal, and La Bombón the opposite: dainty, rhythmical in her walk, with thighs and arms that might emerge from a mold, but repellently vulgar overall.

Rocky is from Villa Clara, and has lived for the past four years in Centro Habana, in La Bombón's room. To cover expenses they consort with foreigners. Right now Rocky is expecting the fifth visit to Cuba of a Spaniard who's been desperate over her from the first. La Bombón broke up with her long-standing Italian, but she won't have trouble picking up a replacement, even if he's Latin American instead. They prefer men; according to La Bombón, a foreign woman is very hard to snag, and they're scarce. Besides, it's always easier for a woman to deceive a man than to deceive another woman. (I don't agree, but I don't say.)

Past midnight somebody proposes the bottle game. There are seven of us. We agree, unanimously, and sit in a circle on the floor. Nancy is in charge of spinning the empty bottle of Havana Club. The first time it points to Virginia, and all of us ask her something daring about her sexual life. That's how it always is: People don't want to know about anything else.

I bend to the expectations of the group. I ask about sex, first Virginia, then Nancy, then La Bombón. The bottle will point at me too, and I'll be peppered with the same. My turn comes.

Soledad takes an interest in details of my relationship with Jorge Ángel. I tell the truth, my answers are like tics: We're lovers, he attracts me, he's marvelous in bed, he's in love with me. No, Claudia, that's obvious; what Soledad wants are details. They push me into lies. I try to evade the details, but once pushed I bombard my listeners to the point of naturalism. I see myself describing things with absolute precision and clarity, I believe it's the truth, assume my fictions, now no longer fiction at all. I invent so much and so vehemently that the sordidness of the world I create is believable and impressive. All of them are listening. I'm fascinated to have an audience, to rule over one. In my telling, Jorge Ángel and I were a special couple, distinctive, yet still something pushes me to make us recognizable within that pack of falsehoods. That kind of lying always passes for the truth. I live by those lies.

Laura believes me, innocently ignorant of my game.

Nancy is interested in Laura, in whether we have slept together yet, in whether I'm in love with her. I protest: That's two questions, not one. La Bombón decides to take the second one as hers. I don't agree. Rocky convinces me; she takes pains to make clear the favorable impression that I'm making on her. While the rest follow the movement of the bottle, Rocky stares at me. I look in both directions at once, I fear being tactless yet at the same time I'm thrilled. I don't imagine having an affair with Rocky, but I incite her nonetheless. It's exciting to watch her risk her relationship with La Bombón for a stranger. La Bombón has now taken account of the looks Rocky is giving, and too-pointedly pretends not to see.

That's the way it always goes when I become aware of someone's attraction. I can never reject them or give them the cold shoulder; I accept complicity, inflate their hopes. I don't know whether this is shyness, vanity, or having the soul of a tramp, but I enjoy it very much.

Laura and I have never slept together. I lie, spread disinformation. I don't claim to be in love with her, only that she turns me on—and finishing that statement, I anchor my eyes on Rocky, no longer sidewise, straight ahead. I want to be chaotic, to confuse them.

There's no confusion, just shouts of approval. Everybody but La Bombón enjoys the message I've let fly toward Rocky's face. Virginia even claps her on the shoulder, congratulating her. They're cruel. So am I. La Bombón laughs loudly to avoid dying. Nobody asks, they plot the next attack. La Bombón gets up to go to the bathroom, and Rocky follows. I feel a sudden extraterritoriality, find myself among strange beings. I have to go, I say, already on my feet. Nancy pulls me by the arm, but I brush loose. Soledad argues there are still questions pending, I walk toward the door, and as I open it I hear the voice of La Bombón, who has come back: "We're going to make *bombón* pastry, didn't you suggest that idea this afternoon?" Collective laughter. That hurts me. I pretend to waver, shake my head, smile—the last concession—and leave.

Days and then weeks passed without my receiving any response. Fearing my message had not arrived, I recopied it three times from the draft, and sent one copy to each post office box. In about a month, a most beauteous mulatto with dark eyes and a sharp nose appeared at my door. To glimpse the swellings of his body through his tight jeans was terrifying. With the most proper syntax and gestures of almost exaggerated refinement, he asked for me by name and I said, yes, that was I, and then he pulled from his backpack an orange-colored envelope that he placed in my hands. Matilde La Mole was returning my letters. Stupified, I invited him to sit, to drink a glass of lemonade, a cup of tea, a coffee, and to reveal to me who Matilde could be.

He offered no resistence, but took a seat right next to the "story" spread out upon the couch. I felt suddenly embarrassed, fearing he would guess that my curiosity had reached the point that I could recite the tale practically by heart. I swept up the scattered pages in my hand and carried them to the kitchen. Yes, the ending was fantastic, I well knew:

The next day she'll appear in my room with a bottle of doctored alcohol. She'll come to tell me that she likes my tits. If it weren't for my reticence, I would have destroyed the farce right from the beginning. Though I disliked Rocky's surprising nerve, I didn't think of it as a pose, not at all, but rather as her supposed natural incapacity to undertake a romantic conquest any other way. I lacked the wit to respond to the directness of her words. In the face of an openness that I thought was genuine, I lacked arguments I was willing to confess. What I did was to accuse her of vulgarity. Impassive, she defended herself: I don't sugar-coat things; I call a spade a spade; I call the potato, potato, and the skin, skin. Scared to death, I kicked her out of my room. She left to come again, many times. Always to see my tits.

I could have avoided the encounters, hidden on other floors, skipped out of the dorm, or not allowed her in. That would have signified an admission of fear. I was caught in my own game, and tried to accept it with elegance. I hardly left my room, kept the door open, waiting.

In spite of my precautions, Rocky saw through me: You're afraid. You're more skin than potato. You act on that you're tough, but you're chicken. I shot back: I don't put on anything; you don't know me. She brandished her cherished phrase: I don't want to know you. It's too complicated. I only want your tits.

It was all lies, we both spoke without conviction. She insisted on laying siege to me for reasons similar to mine for accepting her glances the night of the bottle. When I had a flash of this suspicion, of the truth, I decided to expose myself. I invited her to say, to uncork the bottle, to touch my tits.

Her nervousness betrayed that she prefered the rejections. She touched me; I felt nothing. She kissed me: nothing again. I told her so, and more: The same thing would happen to her. She pulled away, confirming it. At that moment, Jorge Ángel arrived. If I had let him openly interfere in my life, he would have condemned the company I was keeping, but I'm intransigent where my independence is concerned. Though he didn't share these ideas, he submitted in order to stay by my side. Now he left. Rocky too. She never came back.

Jorge Ángel returned that night and we made love without speaking of the matter. The next day I broke up with him and he didn't mention it then, nor the next day, nor the next. Finally, the last day, he threw it in my face. I like it when a surprising gesture or syllable reveals people's lack of elegance, their incapacity for lying or for silence.

I explained myself without affectation or prudery. We made love, and then I repeated my refusal to continue the relationship. Go away, I said. I think I related this already. All that remains to tell is Laura's arrival. Sudden. It had been centuries since Laura was sudden. She appeared in my room the next day. The next day. Two weeks later. Five millennia before. It's annoying to have to organize this history with recurrent and obsessive citations of the time. It would be more pleasant to let myself be seduced by memories, to describe that unforgettable moment without having to locate it temporally, without explanations, without aspiring to coherence or incoherence. It would be magnificent to speak of Laura without aspirations, without even the aspiration to speak of her. Just to speak.

But that's an impossibility, or at most, if a possibility, a deceptive one.

Laura had arrived from Camagüey to offer herself to me, definitively, beyond the shadow of a doubt. She showed me her nails, announcing she was letting them grow again; she suspected my strategem of losing the game and didn't want to participate in something so absurd after this encounter. Now she would sit down with me, face to face. Forgetting the length of our nails, she would accept symbolic defeat and recount her latest sexual experience.

She had had it with a girl, a good friend of hers, a very dear friend, the friend she'd shared a bed with in her high school years, her virgin and sexually timid friend who had suddenly begun to know and experience everything avidly and euphorically, who had become a walking Kama Sutra in fact. That girl had always been her confidante, her attentive ear, her balm and her balsam; and suddenly, she no longer was, and Laura felt her friend slip away among so many other bodies, and she thought that to regain her she had to be one body more, someone else. Perhaps that adolescent attachment, that idyll, hid other longings, other attachments, a deep silence.

Nonetheless, when Laura undressed, and she touched her and they kissed, Laura felt that too wouldn't resolve anything, because the girl still behaved with a frighten-ing coldness, Claudia. It was worse. That's why I'm here speaking frankly with you, girl. Claudia. Dear friend. Ear. Balm. Balsam.

I hugged her. I hugged her, I hugged her; all I can say is that I hugged her. Minutes went by in that embrace.

To reciprocate her frankness would perhaps have been healthy at that moment, but it would have meant a retreat, ruining the little that I had accomplished, and I would have to pay for it later on. More. I changed everything. I lied with elegance. I sentenced her, I humiliated her. I told her I'd known other friendships, another world, fuller, realer: She had remained behind,

behind, lost forever; she was just a memory. I said making love had demonstrated our incompatibility, the emptiness, the distance. She cried a long time, she slept that night in my room, in another bed, and in the morning she left.

Tomorrow I'm going to Camagüey. The only welcome thing would be her, for her to be awaiting me in the train station, almost naked. We'd kiss effusively on the cheek, we'd embrace slowly and tightly. At home, she'd talk about Carlos, we'd show each other our nails, I'd lose and go on lying to her about my happiness, avenging my impotence; I'd describe the sex act between Rebeca and Alicia as if I were Alicia. And so on.

But tomorrow won't be that way, it will be as if I didn't go to Camagüey, and I weren't me, and I never had been.

As if.

Seated now, over our drinks, the mulatto confessed to being a dancer like the character in "The Letter," a story that had captivated him. He had seen me several times in the street and at a few parties, but he never imagined that I might be the author. One day, while waiting to enter the Trianón cinema in the midst of an enormous fluttering of fairies, a youth knocked his floppy sun hat from his head while trying to touch me on the shoulder. Didn't I remember that broad-brimmed ladies' hat? They were showing Almodovar's *Law of Desire* and he had turned transvestite for the occasion; that day he was a blond—a trick, don't ask how. Didn't I remember? And that youth, was he my friend or my partner? No, don't answer, that was an indiscretion on his part. He was obsessed with me. He was drawn toward men like me, he'd been investigating me in our circles until he knew almost all there was to know, but after a hopeless search for a means to approach me, he had decided on one: He was Madame

Rénal, Matilde La Mole, Julien Sorel. He wrote as a hobby, and of the beings he invented, he prefered the dykes. Had Claudia's story interested me? He knew it was no great thing, but that didn't matter, he'd used it only as a pretext to enter my world. He'd read only "The Letter." Didn't I have other pieces? Why didn't I publish them? His intuition told him that behind the hand that wrote something like that, breathed a wild and passionate man, an extraordinary lover.

To say that I was paralyzed by surprise is a necessary convention in this kind of a tale. I was paralyzed by surprise, even if I'd guessed that the mulatto was Matilde since I saw him at the door. He attracted me, but it was impossible for us to go beyond that conversation. He knew everything, even the events with the guy who had sung me that Amanda Miguel song, who was a friend of his who sang the same song to all the boys.

Matilde knew the majority of my supposed characters. That was a danger. Faced with his historiographic expertise, I was forced to recognize in my work a species of cloaked and twisted memory, snippets of autobiography sold off as fiction. Matilde made me feel like the worst writer in the world.

While he proceeded with his recitation, with me as the subject, I considered the disadvantages of rejecting him. If he took revenge by advertising what he knew all over Havana, the success of my book could suffer. Certain labels would forever accompany me. Memoirist. Realist. Et cetera. Et cetera. At that moment Matilde's missives and story took on another color: clever attacks on my "literature," subtle blackmail to gain easy access to my body. No, it couldn't be that bad, all he had read was "The Letter." Perhaps he wasn't really a dancer and, by pretending to be, invented another point of coincidence with the story so as to mock me. No, paranoia was making it difficult to think clearly and astutely. To hell with that foolishness. The solution was simple: stay on good terms with my body and with literature too. Go to bed with Mathilde and then write the story from beginning to end, without adding or subtracting anything. A master stroke. Nobody would believe it had all really happened.

I fit my actions to my plan. I made love with Matilde, with Madame Rénal, with Julien Sorel—the best. Before he left I suggested, as a joke, a title for his text: "How to Act in 1830," Stendhal's title for one of the chapters in *The Red and the Black*. "It's perfect, honey," he said, as his stirring lips parted around his prodigious teeth. "But Claudia has nothing to do with Matilde," he added, cutting the smile short. I felt such coldness that in the doorway I urged him to return whenever he wanted: I had broken up with the beautiful youth who had tumbled his sun hat in the cinema. I was in need of a sustained affair, and if it was with a lover of my stories . . .

He never came back—not even though, in addition, I promised to read him the rest of my book.

Images, Questions Re: Beautiful Dead Woman

TO NUMBER ONE

You would have been less surprising on a bench on Calle G at midnight. You would have been one among many, and I would have chosen you, or maybe not, for there would have been time to mull it over, time to doubt. Instead, I had to be turning the corner, close up against the rough surface of the wall. You had to appear on the far edge of the sidewalk, sudden and imminent, turning toward Paseo as well. I had to be assaulted by visions, to judge you beautiful, to step along with reckless eyes fixed upon Beauty so accessible and free of charge. And Beauty herself began to call me, with oh-so-cautious winks like camera flashes, involuntary but flashes nonetheless. At high noon.

TO NUMBER TWO

You weren't beautiful. It was sun, sweat, and distance. As we drew closer and you ceased to be just a shape, I could see more and more clearly the slackness of your muscles, your lips that could barely contain those imposing, protagonistic gums. And your strange inability to fully extend your thick and curving arms. But I accepted the hand you extended toward me in the middle of the block, counterfeit old friends.

If I had looked at the other pedestrians, I would have read in their indifference how efficiently natural that act appeared. No change in their gaits. Gracelessness, opacity, amnesia. The sidewalk below, the park ahead. All unchanged, if I had looked.

I did look when you proposed that we stop for a glass of juice, and I had to change course, turn around, go with your flow. If everything had been different and some sign of alteration in the rest had unnerved or inhibited me, impelled me toward pride or terror (a little paranoia never hurts)! But "the rest" were others, and other than us. No witnesses, then: we had immunity; we were imperceptible, we were the same.

TO NUMBER THREE

The date, fixed with the morbid exactness of a commemorative event. Paseo and Línea. Nine at night. In the darkness, wooden bench.

A kiss? A brushing of dry, barely open lips. Sharing this blend of ignorance, fear, and first-time-strangeness with another mouth, letting ourselves slip into it: as fluid and shapeless as mercury, or almost falling into a pose.

If you wanted to impress me, that was a risky way to do so in *fin de siecle* Havana. Someone else would have bit into your lips, treacherously, and later would have left. Either you were irredeemably nuts or my behavior was ethereal in the extreme. The latter bothered me more because, in that case, it was my responsibility to change the image. Any gesture, a quick phrase, a furtive hand, whatever. So many possibilities and I didn't try a one.

Luckily it was you. You proposed that we go walking and we ended up, by force of gravity, in the bleachers of Martí Field. The muscular kisses required by the occasion: saliva, emphasis, teeth, lack of air. Standing up, our clothes folded to the left of us. We didn't undress with the violent desperation seen in certain films nor the slow lyricism of others. We undressed in your way, did it all your way: realism to the point of eroding the most minimal certainty. It seemed we were always in transition toward something unknown and unimaginable, where certainty would constitute an absurd rhetoric, where my experiences of kiss, caress, sex, pleasure, and so on were merely concepts, precarious and inoperative ones.

I'm trying to say you were unique. Trying not to deceive myself too much.

TO NUMBER FOUR

Till then, nobody had sunk his teeth into my skull. You, though, slipped from my lips to my jaw, from there to my ear and onward around my head. My body twisted and swiveled in search of some other space, but there was no place for the pliant swaying thing which it became under the pressure of your mouth. An easy metaphor: the writhing of a snake. I moved down one step, feet tentative, eyes out of orbit, unable to reciprocate with the most minimal caress. Supreme passivity. I don't know whether it was self-effacement or selfishness or both at once. Wholly subject to your verdict. Or you to mine?

From my head you descended to my ear, my neck, my chest. Bent down: abdomen, genitals, thighs. Concentrated: penis. I trembled. On the edge of spilling, and your face suddenly deformed, you stopped to request: "Come down here too." Beautiful photo, both of us kneeling there.

Languor. You took my face in your hands, smelled my hair, traced my nose with the tip of your own, touched my lips with your fingers. It was so dark I can't say for sure that you tried to look me in the eyes, but had you done so, it would have passed unobserved and added a grace note to the whole.

After a while you put my head on a level with your cock. "It's yours. Destroy it," you declared.

TO NUMBER ONE

Timidity or cliché, at the moment our paths crossed we lowered our eyes. At the end of the block we turned our heads, each toward the other. Last flash. We smiled. Wasn't there time, or daring, or desire for more?

TO NUMBER TWO

It was an exquisite dialogue:

"You're something. How did you know I wouldn't pass up your hand?"

"I was confused. I didn't know what to do, how to tell you that you turned me on."

"And the juice?"

"Confusion again."

"Your states of confusion are dangerous."

"I think so. Right now I don't know an elegant way out of this situation, and all I can think of is inviting you to my house."

"I accept but on one condition."

"What?"

"That you stay confused when we get into bed."

TO NUMBER THREE

There never was a bed. Sitting in the bleachers we looked out at the sea, the deserted seawall, the sun threatening to rise. I said I was cold. While you mumbled something about the night hours, the dawn, and the temperature, you held up the sleeve of your shirt so as to put my arm in it and you did the same with the other sleeve and your arm. Enough cloth to reach from our shoulders to our knees. I could lean my face against your neck, close my tired eyes and open them for quick intervals, give myself over to an inappropriate lassitude.

Sleep in the morning, write in the afternoon, see you at night at Paseo and Línea and walk toward Martí Field, dawn. I quickly got used to that cycle which you tacitly imposed.

You began to wear an enormous backpack containing two sheets, a pillow, and some newspapers. I don't know what you were before me, whether a *rocker*, a *freak*, or a *hippie* — you must have been one of these. When I said that, you told me a hippie but bourgeoisified.

We rarely made love lying on the blue sheet. Lying down was conversation, covering ourselves with the other sheet, the white one, resting our heads on the pillow, caresses, so I could learn the truth about the mercury and the almost-pose. Excitement was standing up, violating every perimeter, moving, running, hitting, wounding ourselves against the concrete edges, falling, holding, sliding, staining ourselves with dirt. How exactly was it? I try to be pornographic and I can't. It was madness and it was death.

TO NUMBER FOUR

You were neither madness nor death, but their doubles. I outdid myself in convincing you to go to Martí. Faced with such insistence you asked whether I'd been there other times. When I told you about my history with Him you accused me of Nostalgia and Obsession. First reports of an approaching stranger are determining: these intuitions erode or shape everything. I knew that your aggressively clear judgments of me would do the former, but I let the impression slip away, as an intentional error of the fingers lets a disagreeable photo slip from the album. Then you projected those two precise words. Lucidity kept you from living.

Impossible for you to forget the nurse. At least your ghost had an ordinary job, so he could be designated without falling prey to the plague of proper names. I would have had to call mine the ex-hippie and, on top of that, add bourgeoisified. Too long and perhaps contradictory, I thought. I didn't say it, just diverted your attention from nostalgia by vomiting jokes, brilliant and evasive words. You would recall that the nurse was matchless in bed and I would smile. "I'm matchless in the bleachers, and that's good enough, don't you think?"

TO NUMBER ONE

From that day on I found you everywhere in the city, as if Beauty were starting to exist for me. We'd look at each other and pass on by, turn to look again and smile with a complicity that filled me with worry and with joy. At first I would have liked to approach you, but then that desire began to fade. I came to believe that the repetition of our actions had an end in itself, drawing nothing behind or after it.

One day, just after leaving Martí, he and I bumped into you. It was difficult for me to act out our ritual. It cost me a horrible argument. I had to explain something to him that I might never be able to explain. I ended up talking about the Japanese episode in the film *Love at Twenty*—in fact, misrepresenting it. How to tell him that the protagonist loved the beautiful woman and that the other one was so ugly? He would have taken my analogies poorly. But I did put special emphasis on that fact that, in the end, the guy killed the beautiful one.

TO NUMBER TWO

A lot of tea, a lot of rum, a lot of marijuana. Vibrators, condoms, and creams. Magazines, photos, and a video which showed you naked and masturbating alongside beefy youths who little by little began an interchange with each other and with you.

I hallucinated a long, long tunnel through which I slid without my feet touching anywhere. The speed of my body varied, sometimes increasing to the point of nausea and blindness for me; sometimes, in calmness, there was a certain viscosity to the movement, which allowed me to open my eyes and see you above me or alongside or underneath.

I don't know how many hours I was making love, or how. I remember everything being soft or seeming that way; my skin was not my skin but an echo of the tunnel, or of your salients and depths. Some time later I realized you were a nurse.

TO NUMBER THREE

The policeman in the first row of the stands; ourselves, almost at the top. We'd just finished dressing and you were gathering up the sheets, pillow, and papers. I'd like to forget that fear, the halting descent, the identity cards shakily extended, the answers in the form of lies.

I wasn't anything; you were the writer there. According to the story we were cousins, why not, look closely at the father's name of one and the mother's name of the other: Martínez for both. He had just had a violent argument with his mother, who raised the roof over his string of women, a different one every day, so he'd come to stay at my house, but there it was even worse, his women and mine too. My mother — that's his aunt — couldn't handle it either. Now, first thing in the morning, we were off to the station to try and catch a bus for Oriente, where we had an uncle who would help us out. We'd been on the waiting list for two days, it was the weekend, the situation with transport out that way was really bad ... We'd tried to go to sleep across from the station, in the sports center, but a policeman wouldn't let us and, after one problem and another, this was where we'd ended up.

You, not me, were the brilliant writer. The policeman slapped you on the shoulder. He was after the queers who came to the area to do what they did. He gave us back our documents and we left.

The stiffness that my joints had assumed, in feigned toughness, lasted as far as Línea. All the way down the block I felt the policeman's stare riveted to my back.

TO NUMBER FOUR

Leaving Martí I told you the story of the policeman. You skewered me with the word "obsession" again. You couldn't understand how, after such a terrible experience, I would take you back there. "No more symbols, no more symbols," you repeated.

As an order, talking to yourself. Always, you'd start off addressing me and end up in monologue. Conversation was a pretext for wallowing in memories, each in his own.

There was no danger. After that night, they'd put lights in the stadium which lasted a month at most. The couples broke them, and then nobody saw to getting them replaced. The police obsession with Martí Field passed quickly, and now things were back to normal again. So I wound up my defense: "Cuba is a country of waves; they come, they flood, and then they're gone."

"Until the next wave comes," you replied. I was sure you weren't referring strictly to the question at hand, your mind was weaving something thicker and more tangled than that. Metaphors were noxious, they took you even further from the two of us. You. The nurse. Me. One wave and the next. Me. Him. You. "Too aquatic, these associations," I thought, hoping some wit could repel the weight of ill-humor creeping over me. Lucidity kept me from living, too.

TO NUMBER ONE

From the opposite sidewalk you raised your hand, rubbed the air with your palm, and then winked as you bent your head. I responded, surprised by that variation. You instituted a sign of greater contact just when I was starting to feel more distant and would have preferred you to disappear because you were bringing me trouble with him. I remembered the Japanese story. Everything had changed, although, giving it a good second look, there was never any commonality between us and the film. My association was silly.

But was it really? The protagonist killed the beautiful woman to exorcize his fantasies, the imaginary and impossible world that he had erected around his own. Wasn't there an unconfessed sense of impossibility in our glances? Couldn't I have longed to go further but, judging you hesitant, accepted the limits you set, tempered my aspirations, learned to enjoy this resignation and called it custom or rite? Didn't the change in your greeting cheer me up?

TO NUMBER TWO

It took only a few minutes of conversation between you and him for me to realize that you were the famous nurse. There was no sign in your face or in your voice that you remembered me. Were you the man with whom, years ago, I had a hallucinatory affair for the space of one day, one night, a few hours perhaps? Were you the shadow that haunted him? Where was he, while you and I were together? Did he exist, were you unfaithful to him with me?

And so what? One after another, my questions awarded me an intuition more powerful than all the answers: Time, its absolute greed, its authority.

I let myself be led. It was your house. You. Everything the same. Time did not exist, which had to be false. Really, you didn't recognize me? And again, so what?

Flow. Flow. Flow. A lot of tea. A lot of rum. A lot of marijuana. Vibrators, condoms, creams. Magazines, photos, videos. The same. What was time? Who were we? Rhetoric. I searched for the tunnel. Something had changed, better not search at all. Now there was no tunnel, but a flying carpet. You, I, and him, silk, caressable.

TO NUMBER THREE

"Misfortunes come in twos," my grandmother and my mother say. We always end up repeating what our grandmothers and mothers say, however much we resist. The phrase sticks there, in some hidden and buried site of the memory, and then suddenly emerges with a will of its own. Difficult situations come loaded down with ordinary sentences, those are their clothing, the way they present themselves. "Misfortunes come in twos," I said.

A whole week waiting for you on a bench at Paseo and Lìnea and you failed to appear. Fired from the publishing house for repeated absences. Grandmother and mother complaining without letup. No money. No food. Existential crisis.

There's always one misfortune more terrible than the others: your loss. That absolute priority made me feel I was disturbed, or defective. All the rest could go to hell; it was better to have no family, to dedicate myself to loving you, and waiting for you. Didn't I love my mother, what would I feel when she and my grandmother died and I was left alone? What did loving someone mean? It seems simple.

It could be that the explanations about him and the Japanese story didn't convince you, and the suspicion of something hidden induced you to disappear out of fear and pride. Or you needed Martí too much and couldn't tolerate the idea of staying away for awhile until the police wave passed. It could have been that you got caught in the symbols, you just got tired.

TO NUMBER FOUR

Arms around each other's shoulders we exchanged ephemeral kisses, while the odd-man-out of the moment watched. Minimal procession, arriving and falling into bed. I'm not sure what expression or gesture led me to the nurse's head, but I bit it as you had shown me how to do. I don't know whether it was your nose that explored my back, whether that was your tibia, or whether the mouth (liquid as far as the throat), into which my pelvis sank and stroked was my own. Who tried to separate the bones of my right hand with his teeth? Who assaulted my chest with a knee, thinking perhaps it was my rear? Whom did I almost suffocate facedown against the mattress suddenly without a sheet, with expressionistic and botanical arabesques, indecipherable black against the ancient, rough, stained yellowness of its fabric.

I awoke on the floor, chin between two thighs, a fetus in underwear on the magenta carpet. The two of you lay naked in the bed, your breathing soft and rhythmic, and tender, I think. I found my pants in a corner of the bedroom, my socks, shoes, and shirt in the living room. I understood why, in the movies, on the morning after, certain characters don't say goodbye.

TO NUMBER ONE

Without your help I wouldn't have gotten inside the theater. They were showing Almodovar's *Law of Desire* and the gay scene of the city was out in force. As if it were a gay pride march, with signs and everything, only lacking the signs.

The police didn't find a peaceful way to clear the queers from the windows, or to move them away from the entrance so the doors could be opened without the danger of a sudden and lethal avalanche.

I managed to get into the middle of the tumult and you touched my shoulder. You reached me your hand over a curly blond transvestite, knocking off her extravagant sun hat which fell onto my face. "Easy, boy, don't worry, it all works out," she crooned her version of the old jingle to smiles and funny faces, as she put the wide-brimmed chapeau back in place.

At a sign from you I got out of the crowd, having trouble believing I was so close. The police, confounded by so much disorder and so much camp, attacked the compact mass of fairies with clubs and gas, and put them to flight: a confused retreat on broken wings.

You came close to my ear to say they would open a side door where a friend of yours was waiting. I couldn't understand the message. Taking me by the hand you led me imperiously and agilely along a hallway. Your sweat. The mulatta in the doorway. The cold of the theater. Your voice in the darkness.

TO NUMBER TWO

When I saw you I would have liked to sneak away. A week

before, he'd called me on the phone to make a date and talk. I refused, it didn't make sense to go on acting as a substitute for others. I wasn't inclined to be your go-between. It was childish to search for someone else so as not to openly confess the mutual passion you felt. I didn't want to know anything about the reasons for that fear and his strategy, nor to learn whether, at base, I was wrong. The morning vision had been plenty eloquent. It was enough.

Now you both came toward me, but I would have managed to hide behind the tall man with the gray boots if a woman hadn't called from the sidewalk of the Habana Libre so my intended shield crossed the street and gave me away.

He pointed me out to you in the ice-cream line. Greetings, the vicissitudes of your attempt to get here to Coppelia, your problems at work, your imminent anniversary as a couple, five years, the party, the invitation. You and I listened. I should have been happy, but no.

TO NUMBER THREE

I didn't track you with the religiosity of the first weeks. Sometimes, walking by chance near Línea and Paseo, I did go up to the bench, now broken, and waited a few minutes. It was an almost unconscious reflex, the indolence of a symbol.

Although I didn't place too many hopes in the new relationship, that fact of having it allowed me to conceive of waiting for you as something ridiculous or absurd.

You went by on a bus and we spotted each other. I died. You shifted your eyes toward him, keeping me company at my stop after the film. The expression in your eyes belonged to one who doubts that the boy would have killed the beautiful woman in the end. Or so I thought; I needed an answer for your absence and that was the one I found.

"Appearances are deceiving." We always end up repeating what our grandmothers and mothers say, what we say ourselves.

TO NUMBER ONE

Friends, just friends, I explained. It sounded silly, like something from a high school girl. You pointed to the evident desire, but I denied it, said it had worn away with time. So you proposed just a passing interchange, no commitment, a night of pleasure that wouldn't interfere with friendship. Not compulsory, of course not, no way. A weak negative on my part. Why not? Demonically faithful to your purpose, you labeled me — with courtesy and suspicion—a scaredycat, a prude, and repressed. I wanted to be friends with someone like that, finding a friend was as hard and as good as finding a lover, and it truly would interest me, but ...

The bus. Him. I told you absolutely everything. You advised me to forget the history with the one and the farce with the other. I didn't agree with the word farce but anyway I agreed, I needed to hear it.

TO NUMBER TWO

Bench on G. Midnight. One you among many. You approached me with the intensity of a stranger, and I agreed; not knowing you was divine. I didn't even have to ask about your eternal lover. Zero guilt. Lucidity keeps you from living, I had recourse to the phrase. I looked for the tunnel, the flying carpet, but something had changed. I couldn't make anything out. I left. Yet I glimpsed an image: him, my friend, allowing himself to be caressed by a wrinkled hand, right now, a trembling erection in room 1714 of the Riviera. For a solid week, that image and another, terrifying, interception by the police in a hallway, in the lobby, outside. From the corner telephone I dialed the number of the Riviera, a very friendly receptionist, the ringing in 1714, the cadenced *hello* of the old man. I hung up, I was paranoid, nothing would happen this time either, bad thoughts bring bad things. Normal, it was normal. I was having a bad trip, I needed to go to bed and sleep the marijuana off.

TO NUMBER ONE

I'm leaving the machine running. I'm trusting that as soon as you get here you'll notice and curiosity will make you check it out. As always, you'll want to know the ending before. That mania of yours is the deck I'm playing with.

I've written this frightful crossword without knowing how it ends, but knowing that today is the day, even if it ends like this, obliquely, in this cowardly form. That's all I dare to do. Only you can decide the protagonist's fate. Tell me whether he has to kill the beautiful woman or not. I'm up for anything.

Me.

The Portrait

Her name will be Ana. She'll be a painter.

His name was Jorge. He was the owner of a '57 Chevy, and a taxi driver.

Their names are Gabriel and Héctor. The former is beautiful. The latter possesses the former.

2

Ana will meet Jorge on the sidewalk in front of the Hotel Presidente one day when she's trying to get two North American art dealers to her room at Ánimas 112. They'll pay the five dollars Jorge charged for the trip in his Chevy, and Ana will, provocatively, invite the driver to visit her when he found himself in Habana Vieja again.

He went the next week, without pretexts, imaginary trips, or last-minute coincidences. She'll have liked his solid, rather hairy body, his manner of speaking which was free and slangy almost to the point of vulgarity, the well-defined hips, the thickness of his hands, his dark hair cut very short, his incipient beard, his long and abundant sideburns, his ears unpierced and ringless despite the current fashion, his torso muscular. She'll baptize him Toulouse-Lautrec but keep this to herself. She'll have liked his sweaty olive skin and the unconcern with which he let the small drops gather on his forehead and the large ones drip from his abdomen and chest. At most, he unbuttoned his shirt and tried to fan himself by flapping the cloth against his flesh. She'll have liked both his primitivism and the assurance with which he exhibited it. She'll like the sort of men considered attractive before the sexual revolutions and feminist movements. She'll adore the feeling of being penetrated, subjugated by a weighty body that covers her completely and takes her to the portals of asphyxiation. Only this will infuse her with the strength to paint, and then drain it out again: a vicious cycle that will ruin her as an artist. "I'm not a painter; I'm one of Toulouse-Lautrec's whores," she'll write in a diary that no one will care to read: it will never appear: it won't exist.

She'll open the door, be truly surprised, and, surprised, will prepare cinnamon and ginger tea because she won't have any coffee. It will be nighttime. They'll be alone. While the water boils she'll rush to examine herself obsessively in the bathroom mirror, the ugliness of her long and skinny face, her misshapen nose, forehead too wide, hair lank and dry, inadequate scrawny neck. She won't resort to make up. She'll tell herself the liveliness of her expression will make her pretty, and with that conviction she'll return.

He asked about the North Americans, and she'll reply that she won't have had any luck, that her paintings won't have interested them. That was when he knew she'll be a painter. A painter. The word didn't suggest much in particular, just a strange image that alighted in his mind: Ana's fingers squeezing a brush, possibly one of those narrow ones that artists used. Ana will trump this image with photographic speed: Ana's hand grazing his member through his pants. She'll ask him to undress right away, explaining that she can't have a relationship with any man without first having seen his cock.

He undressed, but with a deliberate slowness which will only increase her desire; from so much desire, her knees will shake. Her throat will tighten. She'll think she's forever lost her voice. But not her gaze: The intentness of her gaze will tug at Jorge's clothes like mute but constant scratches. The liveliness of his penis during the ceremony of undressing will serve to corroborate the correctness of her choice. A man who did not wonder or doubt. A man who knew how to recognize the fury of her gaze and not reproach her for a coldness that won't exist. Several times she'll write this idea in her diary; she'll be tempted to term her behavior as that of a post–sexual revolutions woman. But she won't write it, nor even think it. She will merely affirm: "Contradictions are what I detest."

Jorge naked was Ana's destruction. Still clothed herself, she'll crawl on her knees toward that destruction, a few centimeters from her mouth. She'll use cushions to put it within reach. She'll moisten it with the tip of her tongue, nibble it with her lips, chew it very softly, suck it, hide it inside herself with the false security that assumes things submerged will disappear. She'll play with this destruction, she'll want to have it and leave it, she'll take it out and discover it again, huge—why will she always have to suppose that destruction is something huge?—and won't dare to touch it for fear of losing the chance to destroy herself. She'll cry.

Jorge tried to lift her up by her elbows, but Ana, reluctant, will resist. She'll go limp. He gathered his strength and tried again. Ana will have to accede, standing up until his penis brushes her navel. She'll feel cool saliva on her belly. She'll beg him to walk around the room.

He moved with astonished awkwardness. (He was a taxi driver acting as a model.) But his penis remained vibrant, bobbing precariously in the air. Ana will dry her tears and, ecstatic, begin to suggest daring positions. At last, twenty poses later, he was required to mount her on the floor in a corner of the room with her head bumping against the leg of an old cane chair.

When Gabriel and Héctor knock on the door, Jorge had come three times and Ana will be anxious to take up the brushes abandoned since her last erotic adventure, weeks ago. She'll have just a vague idea. She'll want to paint her own gaze.

Jorge got dressed in a hurry. Ana will do so slowly. Gabriel and Héctor make their ill-timed entrance without paying any attention to the stranger, as if he did not exist. Jorge left as soon as he was introduced: Ana won't be able to handle the mishmash of lovers and gay friends. After greeting Ana with a theatricality typical of those who haven't seen each other for a year, Héctor comments in a jocular tone on Jorge's flight. Ana will once again defend her separatist conception of the world, and Héctor crafts a riposte:

"That's not a stitch in time saving nine, that's sewing in a new seam every day just in case. That's cheating, is what."

Maybe she'll record this quip in her diary, as a proof of the cleverness of her friend.

To divert the course of the conversation, Ana will ask Héctor about his travels in Spain. He'll answer at length but with the same neutral tone he always uses in front of Gabriel. All that stands out is the Humboldt complex in the Canary Islands: "A place of ours, but without transvestites or transsexuals or effeminate gays; no lesbians either, of course. Four stories around a park that has a neon sign with the emblem of the place: a dinosaur. All four floors are full of discos, bars, porno films, saunas, darkened rooms . . . It's immense, five or six times as big as the Manzana de Gómez."

She won't open her mouth to express amazement. Gabriel remains silent. Taking her hostess role too seriously, she'll want to bring him into the conversation:

"And you, Gabriel, did you miss Héctor very much?"

"Stupid question," she will note. Gabriel misses him very much, he's been missing him since the beginning of their relationship, as if Héctor had been far away the entire time. But that kind of distance cannot be touched, it's more of something you begin to breathe: it's like a dense air that accumulates around Gabriel until it gets in the way of his breathing, so he grows blind and deaf and loses his capacity to feel distance at all. He grows separate. Living is knowing how distant others are from oneself. The voyage of the one Gabriel loves awards him this privilege of lucidity. It is a relief to know that a real ocean separates him from Héctor, and not that bottomless daily asphyxiation.

"Yes, so much."

Ana will act agitated and vague, and then will tell them that it's time for them to go. As an excuse, she'll cite her muse. Before leaving, Hector takes from his backpack a box containing tubes of paint. Ana will nearly faint from happiness over such an opportune gift. She'll plant a thousand kisses on her friend's cheek and mouth. Finally, when the couple is already on the street, she'll praise Gabriel from the stoop:

"You're as beautiful as ever."

Really this phrase will be addressed to Héctor, and only he enjoys it. He hugs Gabriel tightly around the shoulders as if to say, "You're beautiful, you belong to me." Aloud, he asks, "Did you really miss me so much?"

Silence. The most absolute manner in which we may be dispossessed.

"Really?"

Insistence. The attempt to exorcise silence, that fissure through which we glimpse that the other is escaping us.

"I almost died."

Héctor kisses him on the mouth. He shows signs of wanting to make love.

Making love. Making love is getting naked and asking the master, "Please master . . . lift my ass to your waist / . . . please master make me say, please master fuck me now please / . . .

please master stroke your shaft with white creams /... please touch your cock head to my wrinkled self-hole / please master push it in gently.../ please master shove it in me a little, a little, a little / please master sink your droor thing down my behind / & please master make me wiggle my rear to eat up the prick trunk/please please master fuck me again with your self please fuck me please/master drive down till it hurts me the softness the / softness please master make love to my ass ... & fuck me for good like a girl /... please master make me go moan on the table / go moan O please master do fuck me like that /... please master call me a dog, an ass beast, a wet asshole / & fuck me more violent ... / & throb thru five seconds to spurt out your semen heat / over & over, bamming it in while I cry out your name I do love you / please master."

In Spain, Héctor has read a long poem by Allen Ginsberg; he has recognized himself in a few lines, he has copied them, he remembers them as if those fragments were really the whole poem. But he doesn't bring them to Gabriel. In Angola his chief, also his lover, has possessed him like this, brutally, on top of the desk where Héctor has typed so many company reports. The shoving has broken the glass and wounded one of Héctor's thighs. But Gabriel must not read these things, must not know anything about this captain, this master. The first time Héctor and Gabriel go to bed, Gabriel wants to know about the scar. "I fell on a broken bottle when I was a kid." The first time Gabriel goes to bed with a man, that man has a scar. Gabriel asks about it and is deceived.

Making love is, for Gabriel, that Héctor moves in close to him, kisses him, touches him, licks him, goes on kissing him, touching him, sucks him, kisses him, kisses him, oh, and masturbates him. Gabriel is Héctor's mirror. Making love is, for Gabriel, living the experience of this symmetry. How many times has he wanted to break up that image, those reflections? That would be un-making love.

There must be something that makes homosexual eroticism different, Héctor explains without Gabriel ever having asked. Gabriel's kingdom is silence. The superiority of homosexuals over heterosexuals lies in the fact that the former can do without penetration, transmute surrender into tenderness, spirituality, Hector goes on arguing. Héctor's kingdom is insistence.

Héctor is an artisan. He's thirty-two years old. Gabriel studies philosophy at the university. He's twenty. Tonight they make love. What is making love?

"Making love with a man who doesn't think he's making love, inspires me," Ana will write in her diary. After Héctor and Gabriel leave, Jorge came back. She'll embrace him, beg forgiveness for the delay caused by this visit, say that she won't have been able to cut it any shorter than that. She'll show him the gift, she'll caress his cock, she'll divest him of his clothes and ask him to lie down motionless on the couch.

Ana will have a canvas ready, beforehand. She'll dab at it timidly. She'll want to capture the devastating force of her gaze acting upon Jorge's body, not the characteristics of the eyes that produce it. "The drawing has no force, it doesn't work. What I want is not a portrait, not a face, nothing that can be defined. Force has no shape." Will she write that, knowing it is neither original nor completely true? So what? She'll be a whore, not a painter, after all. She'll allow herself any impropriety, any madness: to hurl euphoric brush strokes upon the oh-so-passive cloth.

Jorge slept without uttering a word. Thus asleep, he could be more easily profaned. She'll revel in this defenselessness, examining him will bring her to a fever pitch. Her eyes red. Crying once again. But it will occur to her that it should be more exciting to have him lie in a room with a hole through which she'll be able to watch him without his posing for her. Ana will require the presence of a limit, a barrier; simply knowing that this body does not belong to her will impel her to conquer it. She'll need the thrill of transgression, the pleasure of theft. "Héctor always tells me I'm a fag with tits. I think it must be true." She won't be able to paint any more, she'll cover Jorge with a sheet. Will she be a post–sexual revolutions woman? What should a woman be, after the sexual revolutions? Those thoughts will infect her, fleetingly, but she won't write them down. She won't even have thought them. "I detest contradictions" will be the most oft-repeated phrase in her diary, but she will never explain.

"Were you unfaithful?" Héctor persists with the same question, taking advantage of the moment to lift the sheet from Gabriel and make him display the beauty of his nakedness. Modestly, Gabriel covers himself again. Finally he decides to break the silence.

"Never."

"I don't know whether I believe you," and he lasciviously uncovers him again.

"What is belief? That which does not exist. What exists is the need to believe" (Gabriel's manuscript, *Philosophical Notes*, page 34).

"I want to make love again," Héctor insists, in reaction to Gabriel's muteness.

Neither one desires the other. "What is desire? A belief. Something which does not exist. What exists is the need for desire" (ibid., p. 78).

Gabriel doesn't answer, he surrenders: he goes looking for desire.

3

Ana will tell Héctor every detail of her relationship with Jorge and the need to find the right place to steal views of her lover. In return, Héctor tells her of his affairs with Spanish men, necessarily omitted during his previous visit.

Ana will adore this confessional and enthusiastic Héctor who reveals himself when alone. Nonetheless, she'll ask about the other. Ana will not understand how such a beautiful boy can live as cloistered as women of a century past. Héctor disagrees, argues that Gabriel goes out for what is indispensable, for school. He doesn't even need to go to libraries, because Héctor has brought him books from Spain. Things are bad on the street, Ana; Gabriel doesn't lack for anything, he gives him everything: money, clothes, food.

Ana will be tempted to reproach her friend for his selfishness, but good sense will restrain her.

Héctor remarks that the two small rooms of his duplex apartment, which he usually rents out, are unoccupied now. They are adjoining rooms and spying on one from the other could be arranged. She'll make it clear that she won't have any money, and he offers her the rooms rent-free until the painting is done. Ana will be skeptical of such kindness, will think that Jorge could have felt uncomfortable in the home of two gays, she too will be bothered by having them so close by. Will it be worth risking her relationship with Toulouse-Lautrec for this idea?

Ana will accept, and she'll invent some way to explain the change to Jorge. He believed her.

Gabriel doesn't understand Héctor's sudden altruism, Héctor who is so reluctant to share his space with friends whose need is much more pressing. But he keeps quiet and welcomes the refugees with his usual beautiful and inexpressive face. He can't stand the taxi driver's vulgarity, doesn't understand this mixture of art with street talk, but he keeps quiet. His silence is complete.

Ana will praise the intricate carving on the wall that will separate her from Jorge. He was surprised on first seeing this large room divided in half, and when they were alone he let his bewilderment out. Didn't they come here to be alone, he asked. Yes, but when he was dead from so much fucking, she will stay by herself and paint, in spite of physical exhaustion that way. He accepted all this, still without understanding it. He didn't need to understand.

Through tiny spaces between the geometric figures that will make up this wall, Ana will scrutinize Jorge's body. She'll ask him to sleep naked. He didn't investigate her reasons. The almost ethereal massage she will award his genitals was enough for him to sense that obedience was indicated. Only later, when he was alone, did it begin to feel strange. He looked at the ceiling, the images in the wood, the lamp. What was he doing here? There was something incomprehensible about it all. He had never before been with a woman this weird.

When the word "weird" appeared in Jorge's mind, Ana will inundate the canvas with an intense ochre that will transfigure the tiny splashes of yellow from the first day. Frenetically, she'll advance. She'll uncap another tube of paint: green. She'll hesitate. She'll feel that *something* will be observing her lasciviously from the painting in progress. She'll want to free herself from all her clothing, shamelessly, impelled to do so by *that* force. Might it be her own gaze, which will have begun to present itself? Might her own gaze really exist outside herself?

When the word "weird" appeared in Jorge's mind, he got up, felt the dozens of triangles, ovals, and pyramids that will stand between the weirdness and himself. Almost by instinct, he pressed his eyelash to the varnish. He looked. He saw the painter naked, upright over her easel, her back to him, rocking like a schizophrenic in crisis, throwing paint this way and that. He suddenly felt himself discovered, was afraid, and for an instant he pulled away from the crack in the wall. But the attraction was greater.

It won't be Ana's slender body that will seduce him, but a warm and indecipherable emanation. He began to masturbate while watching Ana because she will be the only concrete available thing. He felt that he too was becoming weird. He imagined other bodies, superimposed them over Ana's. None of them was motivating him. The cause of his arousal was *something else*.

Ana will be hieratic, leaning forward over the easel, her clitoris brushing its leather leg. She won't know what could be exciting her to the point where she'll have to wrap her fingers around the seat. Will she want to make love with Jorge? Will she want to make love? She'll have to seek out Toulouse-Lautrec in order to know. She'll have to seek out someone.

Ana will rise and go slowly, tense and hunched.

Jorge lay down again, with his eyes open and his cock hard and breakable.

She won't look at him.

He didn't look at her either.

She'll feel those repeated tremors.

He spurted epileptic brush strokes.

She and he, for the first time separate, mutually unrecognizable.

Héctor can't get to sleep, sweats, turns on the desk lamp, paces around the room. Gabriel follows him with half-closed eyes, the sheet pulled taut, trapped under his heels and in his fingers. Héctor leaves the bedroom, walks into the hall, stops before the door to the other room. He is aroused. He thinks of Gabriel but in fact he's not thinking of Gabriel. He is aroused. He can't go out on the street, walk, seek amid the darkness. He thinks of Gabriel, he says so many times to convince himself. He goes back, opens the door, approaches him with fury, tears off the sheet, lowers his shorts, tries to suck him. Gabriel is frozen, terrified. His eyes have become two enormous globes, his penis is a fat wrinkle that cannot be grasped. Héctor sits upon him, rubs his anus against the wrinkle which is ceasing to exist. He squeezes against that which no longer exists. He attempts Gabriel's lips, which hardly open at all. He licks them, sloppily. Gabriel shivers. The air conditioning is very cold. Gabriel doesn't speak, Héctor recovers his wits, he dismounts, shuts off the air conditioner, turns out the light, lies down. Gabriel covers himself. Héctor says he had a nightmare.

Ana will separate from the anonymous body which went through her, and will walk, intense and unconsummated, about the room. She'll feel as if *something* is impelling her toward frenzy and exhaustion. If she can't control *that*, she'll end up turning on herself, lacerating her own body. Nevertheless, she'll be helpless. She'll pick up the objects in her path and squeeze them until they threaten to break. The pressure will drive her to stand before the canvas; the idea of destroying it will make her bunch her fingers. "That's a grimace, my hands grimacing," she'll think. No, she must not unleash *that* against her own work. She'll try to preserve the painting by turning it to the wall.

There will be slow relief, and then a sleep-inducing calm. Ana will recognize Jorge, and embrace him. He kissed her, peaceably, like someone who has brushed against a memory.

4

The next morning, when Ana will turn the frame around to resume working, she will experience the same unease. Finding no plausible explanations, she'll wind up accepting the only one in which she's never previously believed: genius. A sensation as strange as *that* could come only from a deep and essential spiritual connection between the artist and her work, and between mysterious cosmic rhythms and both.

"During those days I did not feel like a whore but like a painter; all my sexual energies went into the canvas. My dedication was so complete that I forgot about Toulouse-Lautrec. He was just Jorge. He wasn't even that," she'll be able to write.

Jorge too awoke with unusual appetites. This time, far from feeling worried, he accepted them with pride, as instincts of his own. Their exaggerated shape testified to his virility.

Héctor opens his eyes, having had a fabulous dream about the captain, a dream that might be memory or premonition or fantasy, he doesn't know. Whatever it is, it's good: Héctor doesn't want to let such a lifeline go.

Gabriel remains tense, stretched and stiff like the night before, suffering from a withdrawal which doesn't yet express itself physically. The slightest touch would curl him into a ball.

Jorge, naked, walked toward Ana, endlessly at her easel. He lay his stiffened cock upon her back, along her backbone, and then pressed his body to hers and hugged her from behind, his hands cupping her breasts. Ana will grow goose bumps, but she won't stop handling the brush. She won't turn to kiss him, or look at him, or speak. He exhaled his own hot breath in her ear. Her body will be a string of endless spasms, as she treads the insistent call of the edge. He redoubled his efforts. She'll make the slightest gesture of separation. Without understanding, he obeyed her sudden distancing.

He stepped back, off balance, and right away closed in again, trying to get between her and the painting, but Ana's arm will fend him off. With his meaty hand, Jorge kept that arm frozen in place. At last she'll react, she'll know he's there, know that destruction waited a few centimeters from her mouth. She'll close her eyes in annoyance and open them, almost violently, when she feels this enormous thing beating against her lips. She'll push away with her feet and the easel will fall down. He tightened his hold on her arm still more, and made her straighten up. Ana's fingers will have let go of the brush, which will leave a blue mark on the floor.

She'll argue, speak of mutual respect, of artistic necessity, of insult. He accused her in return of coldness toward him. She'll repeat the same arguments. He stopped, alarmed by Ana's unusual flood of words, and let her go.

Ana will pick up the easel, set it in its place, and sit down before it once more. She'll need a few minutes to recover from the trembling that will render her hand useless. Jorge left the room and stormed down the stairs in a fury. Héctor, dazzled, goes down as well.

Through the living room window, Jorge, seated, tried to lose himself in the ungraspable flatness of the horizon. His eyes and his mind longed for a constancy that could mean whiteness, nullity, stripping away. Impossible.

On his feet, Héctor observes the multiple lines of Jorge's body. Sinuous, precise, and attainable. Héctor ponders the magnificent cloud that emerged from Jorge's waist and keeps him from concentrating on the integrity of the landscape.

Jorge no longer existed. There's just this cloud, no horizon, no real or imaginary space on which to rest or float. There is just this impulse, this faith, these knees on the floor, this famished mouth swallowing the cloud, this lightning tongue, this rain, the triumphal acidity that reaches his stomach.

Whiteness. Stripping away. Nullity. Jorge counted, stubbornly, on the line of the horizon, which little by little was turning blurry and absurd; then he latched onto the windows, which were too clean to deny the image of Héctor kneeling and all-inclusive; then he shut his eyelids; then he didn't know.

"Excessively abstract," Ana will judge her painting in a moment of detachment. Could those shapes without harmony, those live colors diluted by whim to a deathly pallor, translate her gaze? The fear of being wrong will oblige her to continue, because she will find the answer only in her hand, only in its advance.

"Perseverance is fear. Every repeated question, every obsessive pursuit, is guided by the same essential timidity. We are not daring when we interrogate. To ask something is to be trapped in doubt itself; every movement it creates is false, covers an inertia which we are forever incapable of overpowering. And what is life: an affirmative, arbitrary act, or a paralyzing question mark?" (ibid., p. 99).

Gabriel dares to sit up in bed. He crosses his legs until his feet touch the cheeks of his behind. The sheet is a very intimate shawl that falls softly on his solid shoulders. Gabriel is free. He *knows* all this: Héctor and Jorge have gone downstairs, Ana is painting, nobody will be sniffing after his beauty. Gabriel enjoys the privilege of being absolutely forgotten. He does not exist. He'd like to run around the room, dance, hum a tune, perhaps a children's song, ta-da. He has read, or someone has told him, that freedom is that ephemeral joy that comes with oblivion. The word ephemeral stops him—or is it that his desires have suddenly slipped away and made him think of the word?

He flexes his chest, reaches his hand toward the drawer built into the bed, rummages inside it and finds the stick of incense, the lighter, and the Tarot pack. Gabriel *knows* that downstairs, after sucking Jorge, Héctor has stood up and begun to masturbate in front of him. The taxi driver was surprised by the grandiosity of that penis. Outsized and robust. Smooth and uniform. Imperious. Haughty. Gabriel *knows* that Héctor is not purposely posing for the other, in fact a suspicion that Jorge's close examination of his genitals is a reproach, a blasphemy, or a hidden blame makes him turn around. The lobes of his ass are round.

Gabriel *knows* that through the window Héctor fixes his eyes on the exquisitely languid body of Jorge upon the couch, as if it were a horizon that once, in a dream, became tactile and now is just that: memory, sadness, dying captain, horizon stretching toward blindness.

But Gabriel *knows* that Jorge demolished all the landscapes. A storm in motion. Impetuously he advanced, upright and towering, disposed to blot everything out. And he *knows* as well that Héctor, valiant and courteous, bends forward in secular reverence, separates his cheeks with his two hands, and is on the verge of saying "Master" to him.

"Too academic," Ana will judge. Gabriel *knows* that she, against her own intentions, will have outlined an almost perfect cloud on the canvas. "And to think that I've given and risked everything for an image that wasn't my gaze after all!" But Gabriel *knows* that is not the end. Ana will persist. She will commit herself to erasing or perpetuating the image—after asking herself whether in reality her gaze might not be that cloud, and not being able to respond.

"The end is always an affirmative and arbitrary act, the sworn enemy of the question mark" (ibid., p. 112).

Gabriel *knows* that Jorge was sticking it into Héctor, gently, a little, a little, a little, finally sinking it completely into his bottom. Without lubricants, without table, without benefit of supplication or instruction—without Jorge calling him dog, anal beast, wet asshole, or anything of the kind. What is making love? What should it be? What can it?

Gabriel *knows* that when Héctor begins to rub his penis Jorge covered Héctor's hand with his own. Jorge moved from the waist and pushed, aggressively, against the cloud; he passed through it, converted it into a transparent film—a pane of glass in the middle of the room—so thin that he could touch Héctor's convulsive hand that sketched a horizon on the other side.

Gabriel *knows* that the assault of Toulouse-Lautrec's broad and rapid brush strokes pressed violently against that hand, to eliminate it from the landscape and consummate the creation of the horizon—flat, white, possible—with just his own, the only hand. The worst.

"Poetic. Very poetic. False," Ana will judge. Standing back from the canvas, she'll evaluate the cloud, which will be there still, protuberant, permanently attached like a challenge or maybe a truth. Mistreated by the dabs of paint, cracked and dripping, nearly a total loss, but never a loss: always there.

"Primitive. Common. Kitsch," Ana will prolong her suffering.

Gabriel *knows* that Jorge regretted nothing, did not even reflect on the event, but rather turned to imagining with infinite morbid pleasure what had to happen between Héctor and himself later, soon, because Jorge's intensity was great and did not accept delay. He declared: "If I had a cock like yours, I'd be the happiest man in Cuba. I'd have thousands of women. It's really too bad."

Gabriel *knows* that Jorge's envy seems abominable to Héctor. He *knows* that Héctor has sheltered the couple so as to seduce the taxi driver in a preconceived and unalterable fashion: inaugurating him as Master, investing him with the rank of Captain, like one who grants and places a crown of laurel, a toga, or a diadem on the head, body, or brow of a chosen one. (How long has Gabriel *known* this?) And Héctor does not pardon Jorge's assuming the authority to modify and destroy the best and most important acts of the rite. Gabriel *knows* this: Jorge's spontaneity, his absence of guilt and his compulsive bedazzlement by Héctor's penis are all major crimes.

"Fantasy is the opposite of freedom, its irreconcilable antagonist. Fantasy is dogmatic and authoritarian; it admits neither rebuttal nor exception. In its renunciation of questions it appears to be an end, something that brings closure. But it is always a goal, something which must and can reopen. Hence its paradox and pathos" (ibid., p. 127).

Héctor's response is a quip, another riposte that might become famous if Ana were to include it in the diary that won't exist: "And if I had yours I'd be the happiest gay in the world. I'd have nobody but you. It'd be something to be proud of. Isn't it too bad?"

Gabriel *knows* that Jorge didn't utter another word. It was much simpler to pounce on Héctor and possess him, a thousand times. Now, when Jorge embarked on the nth one, Héctor, his back to Jorge upon the granite table, feels he has to stop everything, turn around—inventing his own pane of glass beneath him—and propose to the driver: "I'll pay whatever you ask, even the horizon. Be Master. Be Captain. I'll be Dog. Anal Beast. Wet Asshole. Wounded Thigh."

But giving it for free, and the resulting naked proofs, would go on tormenting Héctor. To give oneself is to expose oneself. Payment is impossible after that—even more so if Jorge was bestowing on him, just then, the deepest kiss, and the first: atrocious, unlawful, defining. That kiss was destroying everything.

Gabriel *knows* that Héctor enters his destruction, stoic and rebellious at the same time, as if the novelty of saliva, of the eyes that disappear and resurge and are lost, of panting that pauses into inexistence, of a caress ever more caring and melancholic, were a density ever denser from which he had to protect himself even though all prevention was useless, because that density was reality, claw-stroke, and death.

"To live out a fantasy is to risk convoking the vacuum: to close a door and open it simultaneously. Madness. One would have to be the door, not the hand. One would have to not be" (ibid., p. 141).

Gabriel *knows* he has not written anything original, not because he has read or heard words similar to his but because they are so obvious that they mimic the echo of an unknown yet familiar voice, of an unobjectionable presence. That does not deflate or distress him. He *knows* he is a beautiful youth, not a philosopher. His manuscript does not exist, only his beauty and his youth. Can there be anything more?

He *knows* too that this gesture, the three cards picked out at random and tossed upon the bed, the so-personal reading he makes of them while the incense burns, are redundant, dispensable. The Empress and the Tower, and the Devil in between. Art, nihilism, temptation. Trap, desire, descent. Dark knowledge, danger, pain. Without shading or elliptical language: incisive, necklace of few but very heavy pearls that forces us to bow the head and fall prostrate upon the ground: golden chain.

Ana paints a disturbing canvas and, under its mysterious influence, peace and order crumble. In the center is the Devil. Gabriel *knows* that someone has written this story, that it's all a mixed-up vaporous repetition of that other story: the portrait of an old man whose eyes were drawn with such excellence that they didn't seem to be a copy; they looked out so humanly from the canvas, they destroyed its harmony. The old man was the

Devil. The portrait passed from hand to hand, sowing anxious, sordid sensations in its owners. At last, someone stole it during an auction.

"Brilliant. It was a masterwork. Losing it meant ceasing to be a painter, meant never coming to exist. From then on I was just one more indistiguishable whore," Ana will affirm a few months before dying, in a diary that will never appear.

"Brilliant. It's a masterwork. I'm a painter," Ana will think as she stands before that disseminated cloud, that grayish un-formed whirlwind laced with the thinnest black inlays and mottled with rough splotches of many hues. She will repeat—a psalm, a chorus—that it is brilliant. Three, five, twenty times. She'll masturbate, babbling this, and fall asleep hoarse.

Gabriel *knows* that he, with the shawl over his shoulders, goes into the room where Ana will be lying. Above the easel the painter will have left her palette and brushes. The youth, more beautiful than ever, wraps his fist around the head of a brush and, while rhythmically piercing the canvas with the point of this improvised weapon, feels the humid paint on the bristles sniffing the palm of his hand. His breathing dictates the fre-quency of the blows. Gabriel *knows* this: The sheet slips off and falls onto the paint-stained floor. He does not retrieve it until the gaze has become extinct, until Héctor and Jorge are paralyzed, one of them facedown on the granite table; the other, Master for only a few seconds, his chest upon Héctor's back.

Gabriel *knows* that Jorge, astonished and alarmed, pulled away from Héctor and ran up the stairs, pounding the cement with a speed that Héctor hears as punches, doors, and endings.

Gabriel *knows* that a long time goes by before Héctor decides to come upstairs too. He trudges up tiredly; the sweat of his bare feet marks the trajectory of this slowness.

Gabriel *knows* that he washes the paint-smeared hand and then drops the sheet into a bucket of soapy water to let it soak until he and Héctor are alone.

At dawn Ana will awake, startled, before the shreds of canvas and the empty frame, and she'll throw herself upon Jorge shaking him by the shoulders and berating him for having given in to such base impulses, having betrayed her so treasonously. Jorge thought Ana had discovered about him and Héctor. It was not worth rebutting anything, or even justifying it; it was better to leave it all behind, to get dressed without looking at her and leave without saying goodbye to anyone.

Gabriel *knows* that Héctor is consoling his sobbing friend, that he helps her to gather her belongings in a backpack, accompanies her to the apartment door, and almost pushes her into the elevator. Sheet of metal. Amputated image. Inexpressive goodbye.

Gabriel *knows* that Héctor returns and that another man, without face or defining characteristics, anonymous, seeks Gabriel somewhere, and stops now, overcome by the rash absence of the youth. That man desires him. There is no silence to immunize them or make them healthy and false. Only the night, Gabriel's tremulous and passionate words, uncoercible like the first babblings of a child; only that truly warm kiss after the words, only their naked bodies, weightless, almost unreal. Only desire, simple and atavistic. That man is the only one who exists.

Who is the other who now comes toward Gabriel? He *knows:* It's Héctor, who comes and sits on the edge of the bed, looks at Gabriel lying there, and cries mutely in front of him. Then he lies at his side and hugs him and still does not speak. Atavistic and simple as desire. Gabriel allows himself to be embraced, and *knows* that the unknown man begins to move, moves away while Gabriel lets himself be embraced, and disappears around a corner. Only the two of them exist, Héctor and Gabriel. Ana will never meet Jorge; Jorge never met Héctor. It's all the work of the Devil. Gabriel *knows* that, he gets up and goes into the bathroom, sinks his hands into the bucket, and scrubs the sheet devotedly.

5

Her name is Ana. She's a painter.

His name is Jorge. He's the owner of a '57 Chevrolet, and a taxi driver.

Their names are Gabriel and Héctor. The former is beautiful. The latter possesses the former.